Iris in *Bloom*

Take a Chance: Book Two

NANCY WARREN

Iris in Bloom
Take a Chance: Book Two
Copyright © 2014 Nancy Weatherley Warren
All rights reserved

Cover Design by Kim Killion

Discover other titles by Nancy Warren at
www.NancyWarren.net

Chapter One

Iris Chance usually had a smile and a cheerful word for every patron of Sunflower Coffee and Tea Company, the café and bakery she owned in Hidden Falls, Oregon. But not this morning.

Dragging up a smile was tougher than dredging hair out of her clogged sink, making small talk even tougher. When she futzed her latte art so her heart looked like a cancer growth, she pushed the mug to her customer anyway.

"What's wrong with you?" Dosana, her helper, asked when they had a lull.

"I found a gray hair this morning, that's what."

"One gray hair? You're acting like the Zombie Apocalypse is upon us for one gray hair?"

She picked up a cloth and wiped down the espresso machine. "And it's my birthday coming up. Thirty-three. It seems so old."

"Thirty-three is not old." Dosana was all of twenty-two so Iris was not inclined to believe she knew what she was talking about.

"Jesus was thirty three when he died."

"But not of old age."

"I know. But look at everything he accomplished." She used her fingernail to scrape a stubborn spot. "I feel like I'm treading water, you know? I think of all the dreams I had when I was your age. And what have I done with my life?"

"Iris, look around you. You own this place. You've built a business. Everyone in town comes in here for coffee and your famous desserts and so do most of the tourists who roll through town. You could totally franchise if you wanted to. Plus, you're a published author."

"A couple of short stories. Big deal." Her mouth twisted. "Okay, I'm being a total bitch. I think my mom had about six kids by the time she was my age. Most of my friends are married now. I thought I would be, too."

"Oh, ho. Is that what this is about? A biological ticking clock thing that you old people get?"

She shoved her employee with her elbow. "I don't know. Maybe."

"Hottie incoming, that should cheer you up."

She glanced up and saw that Scott Beatty was peering through the glass door before coming in. Checking to see that she was behind the counter and not too busy. She was not particularly cheered. "He only wants to cry on my shoulder about his breakup with Serena and tell me how much he misses her."

"That's sweet."

"Maybe. But I don't want to hear any more about their sex life."

"Their sex life? Why? Was it—"

"Kinky. Very kinky."

There wasn't time for more as the door opened, the sunflower chimes tinkling merrily, and Scott walked in. "Hi Iris, hey Dosana."

He strolled toward them in worn jeans with a rip in the knee, a plaid flannel shirt with a gray T showing beneath and sturdy boots on his feet. "Hi Scott, what can I get you?"

He looked at her in surprise as he did every morning. As though he might have wandered in looking for motor oil or a new tractor blade. "Uh, coffee I guess."

"Dark roast, medium roast, latte, mochachino, espresso?" She really needed to get a grip. Poor guy looked ready to turn tail and run.

He blinked. "Could I get a small medium roast?"

After she'd poured his coffee and he'd paid and thrown a dime in the tip jar, he said, "Can I talk to you for a second? If you're not too busy?"

And because she wasn't that busy and she felt sorry for him in all his pain she said, "I can take a few minutes," and sat with him at one of the tables by the window while he poured out his heart to her about another woman. "The thing that really hurts is she lied."

"Yes, she did." Since she'd heard the entire story of the cheating and the lying and the breakup more than once, this was not news.

He frowned down at the coffee as though it were to blame. "I never thought she'd cheat on me."

"I know."

"Not after what we had together. I mean, it was so hot, hotter than anything I'd ever done before."

Oh, not going down that path again. She stood. "I've got to get back to work. But you enjoy that coffee and maybe you should think about getting out there and dating again."

"I guess." He sounded totally dejected.

"Why aren't you going after him?" Dosana asked when she got back behind the counter, bringing some dirty mugs with her. "He's totally hot and he's recently single. Snap him up before some other girl does."

"Because he treats me like a cross between his mother and his therapist, that's why." Plus the kinky sex thing.

"It's because that's how you act. You know that right? Half the people who come in here want to tell you their problems and get you to fix them."

Iris blew out a breath. "I'm the oldest girl in a family of eleven. I can't help it. My whole life I've been the stand-in mom."

"Well, stop it. Start acting like a hot woman who deserves to be wooed and not like their mother."

"You're right."

"I know. Next hot guy who walks in here you are going to flirt."

"The only hot guys in town are already taken." She thought of her gorgeous brother. "Or gay."

"So flirt anyway. Believe me, you need the practice."

Flirting. As if. She hated everything about it: the fake gestures, the smile like every stupid thing a man said was fascinating, the pretending to be someone she wasn't. Any man who wanted to get to know Iris was going to have to take her as she was. Or not at all.

She began to tidy the muffins in the case. They'd done a brisk morning business and now it was almost eleven. She had to decide whether to bake more muffins and run the risk of having too many left over or of not baking more muffins and risk losing a lot of muffin sales.

While she debated, the jingle of the hippy bells her mother had given her as a store-warming gift jangled. She rose and glanced to the doorway.

A man entered with that slightly unsure look of someone entering a place for the first time. He darted a glance around, and then seeing the big chalk board and the case of bakery goods, stepped forward.

He had a slightly rumpled look to him. A nice face, kind of Greg Kinnear looking with brown curly hair that needed a trim, candid blue eyes and a killer smile, which he flashed her when he caught her looking his way.

"Hi," he said.

"Hi." She gave him a moment with the board. "What can I get you?"

"An Americano, two lattes, one latte with soy milk, a jasmine tea and a regular dark roast."

Dosana came out of the back at the sound of voices. "I'll get the tea going," she said. As she walked behind Iris she murmured, "Flirt."

"Are those muffins as good as they look?" He had a good voice, she thought. Easy to listen to.

"They'd better be. I made them myself." Oh, blech. What was she doing? That's why she never flirted. She was no good at it. She sounded like a smarmy tout on the shopping channel.

"Great, I'll take half a dozen."

While she got started on the lattes, Dosana brought over the tea and rang up his order.

Then her assistant grabbed a cloth and went out front to wipe tables leaving Iris alone with her customer.

"Passing through?" she asked. Probably with a wife waiting out in the van with the four kids.

"No. I'm starting a new job. At the high school. I'll be the new English teacher."

"Oh." Because the last one nearly died and she thought it might be best not to bring that up.

"The drinks and muffins are bribes for my new colleagues."

"I hope it works."

"Me, too. If your coffee is as good as everyone tells me it is, you'll be seeing a lot of me."

"We'll look forward to it." She pulled out a cardboard tray and began lidding and fitting the drinks into it. As she bagged muffins, she noticed Dosana and Scott head outside. Dosana had quit smoking. She really hoped she hadn't started up again.

"Geoff McLeod," the new English teacher said. He held out a hand.

"Iris Chance. Nice to meet you." His hand was warm, his grasp firm.

"Well, wish me luck."

"I do. What grade are you teaching?"

"Eleven and twelve and creative writing. I've got my elevens this afternoon."

She nodded, thought of her younger siblings who'd most recently attended Jefferson High. "They'll hate you for King Lear."

"Thanks for the pep talk."

She grinned. "Anytime."

As he balanced his laden tray and the muffins and headed toward the door she ran forward. "Let me get that door for you."

She could hear Scott and Dosana talking. They must be right outside.

"What's wrong with Iris?" She heard Scott ask Dosana.

Before she could open the door that would ring the bell announcing their presence, Dosana answered loud and clear.

"She's feeling old with her birthday coming and all. You ask me, she needs to get laid."

6

Chapter Two

Geoff was still chuckling when he pulled into the staff parking lot at Jefferson High. It wasn't every day you got to see a very pretty woman blush the color of a ripe tomato.

She had the redhead's easy blushing skin. Not that she was a redhead, exactly. Her hair, which she'd worn tied back, was more strawberry blond than red. She had blue green eyes that shone with kindness and a sweet smile.

He wondered why she wasn't getting any.

Not that he had any interest in women or sex right now. Not after what he'd been through. She seemed like a nice woman though. Comfortable, the sort of person you could talk to.

Something had stirred within him when he'd caught her eye after they'd both heard the 'she needs to get laid' comment. An awareness, he supposed, that she was an attractive woman. If he was noticing at least that had to be good. Meant he was getting ready to move on.

He balanced the cardboard tray of drinks and the paper sack of muffins with his battered leather briefcase and backed his way through the double doors that led into his new school.

Some days he still felt like he was attending high school. He was the student who never really left. Just kept coming back year after year. The kids were always teenagers; only he sported thicker facial hair, a thicker chest, and a stodgier wardrobe.

"Hey, Mr. McLeod," three girls chorused as he walked by. Pretty, cheerleader types. All were in his eleventh-grade

English class. He remembered one name. Not bad for three days here. By the end of next week he'd know every name of every kid in his classes. "Hi girls," he answered.

"See you in class," Rosalind said as she sashayed by.

"Uh, huh." That's why he remembered her name. She was the mouthy one. He'd bet money that she'd be the first student who whined about how studying Shakespeare had nothing to do with real life and was a waste of her time. He bet she didn't even know that her name came from Shakespeare.

He walked into the meeting room and handed out the coffees and, since there didn't seem to be a plate, ripped open the bag and left the muffins sitting on the brown paper.

"Oh, yum," Ellen Hampton said. She was the English teacher for the freshmen and sophomores. A comfortable woman who'd been here so long all her three kids had gone through Jefferson high and graduated. "You went to Sunflower like I told you."

"Yes, I did." He knew already that he was probably going to do most things that Ellen thought were a good idea. She had the experience and no desire to move up. She liked her job and had no problem that Geoff had been brought in to head the English department.

There were six of them in the department and, according to the principal who'd hired him, they were a solid bunch. He hoped so. He didn't have room for more drama in his life. He wanted a quiet place where he could lick his wounds. He'd liked that this was a big outdoor recreation area. He needed fresh air, low stress and to be very far from his past life in LA.

He was lucky that a teaching job had come available in mid year. The last person in this position had suffered a sudden heart attack, fortunately not fatal, and decided to retire on the spot.

He hoped the kids weren't responsible for the heart attack.

He'd agreed to a two year contract which he thought would give himself time to get his bearings again since his marriage had so suddenly and unexpectedly imploded. Figure out who he was and what he was going to do with the rest of his life.

He was thankful to get a job mid school year, thankful for the rhythm of teaching. Didn't matter the school, not really, kids were kids and there was an essential rhythm to a high school year that was strangely comforting.

The classroom might be a little more beaten up than in his last school, the technology older, but he'd figure it out.

He brought his poster board quotations from famous authors, his collection of literary action figures. Like a new kid trying to turn a dorm room into his temporary home, he personalized his classroom.

He had his elevens after lunch and he recalled Iris Chance's words, "They'll hate you for King Lear." That was coming up soon, but not, thank God, today. They were currently studying poetry, talking about Emily Dickinson and Walt Whitman.

His next block was creative writing. This was his second session now with these kids and he was almost as bored as they were. How was it possible that an entire class of creative writing students didn't seem to have a single creative idea among them?

After he listened to three students in a row read aloud stilted stories that were as lacking in drama as they were in originality, he gazed around at his action figures and his posters as though the plastic figurines of Jane Austen (weapon, her lethal wit) or Edgar Allan Poe with the removable raven on his shoulder waiting to swoop on the unwary might use their powers on these kids.

The silence of thirty kids shuffling and wondering why the teacher's standing in a trance slowly broke in on him.

He chose a kid at random. Because he remembered his name. "Mitch, would you read the words on that poster right behind you on the wall, nice and loud for us?"

The kid was so startled he sat up straight. Turned and looked behind him. "That one?"

"Yes."

"Uh, 'Don't be too timid and squeamish about your actions. All life is an experiment. The more experiments you make the better.' Ralph Waldo Emerson."

"Thank you, Mitch. What do you think Emerson means there?"

Mitch shrugged his shoulders.

"Anyone?"

"That you should try new things?" a girl said, her voice a question.

He beamed at her. "Exactly. So I have to ask you why you aren't taking any chances at all in your own stories? This is creative writing. Part of our job here is to express ourselves in new and creative ways. To create new worlds or tell a story in a way that evokes an emotion in the reader."

The same girl put up her hand. "Yes. Was it Sarah?"

"Uh huh. Um, Mr. Bennett told us we had to follow the rules of composition. He gave us a text book."

He'd found a copy of that text in the locker where his supplies were kept and assumed it was a piece of school history, not that anyone was actually teaching that crap.

"Okay. I know it's always hard to have a teacher who comes in with new ideas when you're used to the old one, but suck it up. From now on, we do things differently."

A flicker of interest stirred like a breeze over dry leaves.

"First, has everybody seen The Dead Poets' Society?"

Not a single soul had even heard of it.

He made a note. "Next class, we're viewing the movie. In the mean time, you can bring in your copies of the composition book. We won't be needing them again. Instead, I want you to take your stories, every single one of them. Go home and rewrite them."

A collective groan rolled over him like an ocean wave trying to suck him under. These kids had attitude.

"How does that make you feel? Me making you redo an assignment?"

"Pissed," Some boy yelled. Snickers erupted.

"Okay. Anger's an emotion. Work with that. Write about how stupid it is to have to redo an assignment, turn it into a horror story about how the new teacher gets tortured by aliens. I don't know. Even if you read your story over and love it, that's okay. But—" He pointed at the Emerson quote, the old gray haired dude seeming to approve of him as he glanced timelessly back. "Take a chance, like Emerson says. Experiment. In my creative writing class I am more interested in the creative than the rules. Got it?"

"Yes, Mr. McLeod."

"Okay, next class, bring me those stories. Rewrite the story you've got, write something completely new, but go to the edge. Jump over the edge if you like."

"And then we get to watch a movie?"

"And then we get to watch a movie," he promised.

Of course, in that movie, one of the creative kids died and the teacher got fired.

Experiments, he reminded himself, involved risk.

As he walked out of his classroom at the end of the day he felt like he was making headway. He understood that the Mr. Bennett he replaced had been teaching at this school for thirty years. Geoff had a feeling the lesson plan hadn't changed a bit in all those years.

Well, he thought, things were about to change in the English department of Jefferson High.

He was heading for the door that led to the staff parking lot, when a woman's voice called, "Geoff."

He turned and waited as one of the science teachers hurried up to him. Tara. Her name was Tara something. She was smiling at him in a way that made him feel slightly harried. One thing he'd loved about being married was the barbed wire fence of safety it provided. He'd been hit on a time or two and always deferred to the ring. Now he didn't have the protection of the ring any more.

She was a nice looking woman. Hot in fact, with long stylish blond hair. He noticed she liked to wear tight clothes and clingy tops that were barely on the correct side of appropriate. Big smile. Friendly. He tried to convince himself she was only being friendly when she came right up to him and said, "Good, I was looking for you."

She had a Texas accent. "I was lookin fer yew."

"You found me," he said, brilliant creative writing teacher that he was, so good with words.

"Some of the younger teachers head to Eugene on Fridays after work. Have a couple of drinks, sometimes do dinner. We're going tomorrow. I wondered if you'd like to come."

"Oh, thanks. Uh, I only got my stuff delivered yesterday. I'll be unpacking tomorrow. But thanks."

"Well come next time, then."

"I will. Thank you." Then, thinking maybe he'd been too abrupt, he said, "I already agreed to go to a vegan potluck, whatever that is."

She stopped to stare. "You're going to the vegan potluck?" She said it as though he were going to worship Satan. Of course, being from Texas, steak capital of the world, she probably did consider vegans to be in league with the devil.

"Yes. Ellen invited me. Seemed like a good idea to get to know the town."

"Well that's good that you're not sitting home alone all weekend."

She didn't leave his side but walked with him to the teachers' parking lot, chatting the whole way. How was he lahkin it here, did he think he'd stay lawng?

She was a nice woman, friendly. Sexy as hell. And he had zero interest.

He wondered if he'd ever be interested in women again, then recalled that moment earlier in the Sunflower Coffee and Tea Company when he'd felt that flicker of awareness.

Not that he'd be dating anytime soon, but maybe one day.

13

Chapter Three

Marguerite Chance strolled into Sunflower later that afternoon. In her hands was an earthenware pot with paper whites just coming into bloom. A second pot held a robust basil plant, bursting with fragrant green leaves. "Oh, how pretty," Iris exclaimed as she gave her sister a quick hug. "And thanks for the basil."

"Don't kill this one," Marguerite ordered. Iris was sadly aware that she had killed the last two basil plants her sister brought her. "Thought I might trade them for some green tea, a veggie sandwich and," Marguerite breathed deeply. "Oh, tell me that's your wicked brownies I'm smelling?"

"It is. And it's a good trade." Marguerite was magic in the garden and absolutely useless in the kitchen while Iris was the exact opposite. Marguerite grew her herbs for her and kept her small garden tended, while she made sure her younger sister got fed. It worked.

The coffee shop wasn't too busy. A few teenagers who'd come in after school lounged in comfy chairs sipping fancy coffees and goofing around.

An older couple sat at a table with a road map in front of them. She suspected they'd come in to use the washroom on a long road trip and then bought coffees because they felt bad. The fact that they'd ended up having paninis and two of her wicked brownies for dessert she put down to her talent in writing up her food descriptions, cooking same, and displaying it all to advantage.

Other than that, there was a quiet guy named Eric in the corner with his laptop. Eric was a budding screenwriter who worked in the horror genre. So far all he'd experienced was rejection but he'd told Iris repeatedly that he felt like the energy in her coffee shop was really creative.

He'd also taken to pouring out his troubles, both creative and personal, whenever he got the opportunity.

"What are you bringing Sunday night?" Marguerite asked, bringing her back to earth.

"Sunday night? Oh, don't tell me it's a family dinner I've forgotten."

"No. It's the vegan potluck and it's at my house."

"But I'm not a vegan."

"So what. You're my sister and I need you there." She paused to sip her tea. "I also need your pot luck dish. You know I can't cook."

She eyed the pots sitting on the table between them. "I'll make you a vegan dish. Probably containing fresh basil. But I can't face all that tie-dye and hemp."

"Be nice about our parents." She grinned. "It'll be fun. Scott Beatty will be there. And maybe some other single guys."

"There are no decent single guys in this town."

"There's a new teacher at the high school. He's coming."

Now her interest was caught. "Geoff McLeod is coming to the vegan potluck?"

Marguerite put her cup down with a snap. "You know him?"

"No. He came in this morning and grabbed some coffees and muffins."

"And?"

"And nothing. He seemed nice. He also seemed married."

"I don't think so. Nobody mentioned a wife."

"Maybe she's, I don't know, packing up the house or something and coming out later."

"You can ask him all about his wife at the potluck. Sunday."

The trouble with owning a coffee shop was that everyone in town knew where to find her. And, even if she tried to shut herself away in her kitchen at the back it didn't matter. The number of people who felt they had the right to barge back here astonished her.

Her mother being the worst offender.

"Hi, darling," Daphne Chance said, appearing at Iris's side while she cooked up an experimental vegan dish in her kitchen. "I didn't see you out front so I thought I'd sneak back here and see how you're doing."

"I'm doing fine, Mom. Trying out a new recipe for brownies made with beets. For the vegan potluck."

"Oh, that sounds delicious. I can't wait to try them."

Actually, neither could Iris. She liked adding new menu items and seeing how they went over. There were enough vegans and food sensitive types in the area that she thought she might try selling the beet brownies if they turned out okay.

She also made a dish of brown rice with garbanzo beans and coconut milk and various spices (including fresh basil) that was quite delicious. At least she wouldn't be too hungry.

When Sunday night came, she dressed with care and knew she wasn't doing it for Scott Beatty. Even as she stood in front of the mirror to push the silver posts of her favorite amethyst dangly earrings through the holes in her ears she saw the excitement shining in her eyes.

Okay, so there was an interesting new man in town. And she liked the look of him. He'd been in again Friday morning on his way to work and they'd exchanged a quick greeting. She'd taken the time to note that he wasn't wearing a wedding ring, not that lack of a ring was evidence of being single. She'd find out for sure tonight.

Not even the humiliation of knowing he'd overheard her assistant announcing her lack of a sex life could quite prevent the flutter of – something, when she thought of him. Maybe, if nothing else, she could sharpen her flirting skills.

Iris finished dressing. Because her work required clothes that she could wear to cook and serve food, when she went out she tended to dress up a little. She wore her good jeans, the ones that were figure flattering, a sleeveless white cotton shirt and a few silver bracelets and the rings she never wore at work.

She put extra effort into her makeup, actually bothered with her hair, styling it in loose curls that hung past her shoulders and decided she was good to go.

She packed up her casserole dishes in her hatchback and headed to her sister's house. While she'd chosen to live in the city of Hidden Falls, in a tiny house built at the turn of the century, back when the town enjoyed its boom as a logging town, her sister was more rural.

Marguerite's little piece of heaven was a corner of the land that their parents lived on. It wouldn't work for everyone, but it worked fine for Marguerite. She had land to grow her vegetables on, quiet which she seemed to crave, and yet her family were all close by.

The vegan potluck had been started by a small group of vegans and grown to be a monthly event that drew a lot of people. Carnivores, omnivores and vegetarians were all welcome. But the same open mindedness did not extend to the food people were allowed to bring to the potluck. In fact, there was a list of instructions that went out each month with the reminder emails. No eggs, no dairy, no honey, which she always thought was going a tad far.

Didn't matter what she thought. The rules were the rules. Each person was required to bring a potluck dish that would feed six people and include a list of ingredients and the recipe.

Baking brownies without eggs was a challenge but in baking Iris loved a challenge. Her beet brownies were surprisingly good. Rich and dense and, because she'd used good chocolate, bursting with dark flavor. She was less thrilled about some of the dishes she'd be encountering at the potluck but at least they didn't frown on alcohol, so she could enjoy a glass of wine and hang out with her friends and neighbors.

She was enjoying her first glass of wine and chatting to Reyna Moore. Reyna was her accountant and the accountant of most of the small business owners in Hidden Falls. She and her husband boarded horses and offered riding lessons on their ten acres, and they had three kids that kept them busy. They were standing in the big open living area of Marguerite's small house and, during a pause in the conversation, she glanced up and happened to see Geoff walk in, following the instructions on the big note taped to the door that said: Don't knock, come on in.

As he did she felt his aloneness. Had an instant instinct, not only that this was hard for him, but that there was an invisible woman beside him as obvious as a missing limb.

18

She watched him glance around, felt the warmth of compassion begin to flow through her. He held a salad bowl and even though she knew she was doing it again, that thing she'd sworn not to do, her instinct to nurture and protect was stronger than her ability to flirt.

She excused herself from Reyna, feeling that being Marguerite's sister gave her an excuse to act like a hostess. She strode forward. "Hi, Geoff," she said, and took the bowl from him. "I'm—"

"Iris. I remember." No doubt they were both hearing the silent 'the one who needs to get laid.'

"You made it. And you brought food."

"I brought salad. I drove to Eugene to get vegan salad dressing. I didn't want to risk compromising the vegan guidelines."

She chuckled. "Come on, I'll show you where the food goes."

She led him through to the dining area off the kitchen where a line up of various casserole dishes, plates and bowls contained everything from kale slaw to nut casseroles to her beet brownies.

She made a space for Geoff's salad. "Would you like a glass of wine?" she asked.

"Is it vegan?"

"Of course."

"Okay, then."

She poured him a glass of red and topped up her own glass.

"Come and meet everyone," she said taking him under her wing without even realizing she was doing it.

The crowd wasn't all hemp and tie-dye. A few of the women in particular dressed up.

He had a nice way with him. He was friendly, able to make conversation with anybody but she noticed there was always a slight distance as though he knew that he could end up on the other side of a parent-teacher conference with any of these people so he didn't let himself get too cozy.

They were called to order by Hal Gerome, a soft spoken man who ran the local health food store and offered meditation retreats and yoga classes in the back of his store. "I'd like to welcome everyone to our feast." He held out his two hands. "Now, if we could all join hands, let's share a blessing before we eat."

She glanced at Geoff to see how he was taking the blessing and found him looking down at her with a tiny twinkle in his eye. He held out a hand and she put hers into it. Why should that feel intimate? It was ridiculous. Her other hand was taken by Barbara Mirkowitz who, everyone in town pretty much considered a saint. She and her husband had retired here with little money and what they had they tended to give away. Barbara rode her bike in all weather all year round, wearing a string of battery operated Christmas lights around her neck to make her more visible on the roads. When they'd discovered a homeless woman begging, they'd invited her to pitch her tent on their property.

But Barbara's saint like hand did not make her sizzle on contact.

When everyone was joined in an approximation of a circle, Hal asked everyone to close their eyes, "If that feels right to you." He gave them a moment and then he gave a blessing that was more of a standing meditation than a prayer.

After that, it was time to eat. Geoff stayed loosely by her side as they chomped on nut casseroles, rice and bean dishes, various dips and breads and salads.

At one point, they were alone and he leaned in. "I have a confession to make."

"Really?" And here's where he tells you his wife will be following with the U-Haul in a couple of days.

He leaned closer. He really did have the nicest eyes, blue with enough flecks of gray to keep things interesting. "I'm not a vegan," he said with great seriousness.

Oh, he was definitely hitting on her. In that moment she became convinced that no wife in a U-Haul was going to show up. "Neither am I," she whispered back.

"Does that mean if I were to ask you out for a burger you'd go?"

"Are you asking me whether I eat meat or are you asking me out on a date?"

His eyes squinted briefly. "I am so out of practice. I'm asking you to have dinner with me. Do people still date?"

"I believe it's still a common custom."

"Will you? Go on a date with me? Have dinner with me?"

She recalled the way he'd walked in as though an invisible partner were by his side. "Are you single?"

"Yes," he said sounding shocked that she would ask. "Of course." He added, sounding less certain. "Barely," he finally admitted.

She nodded. Who knew the signs better than she did? "Long term relationship?"

Sadness swirled around him like a sudden, cold fog. "Marriage. Ended."

21

"I'm sorry."

"Thanks. So am I." Then he seemed to pull himself together and remember that he was talking to a woman he'd asked out on a date. "You seem nice, like someone I could talk to."

Of course she did. He was going through a tough time and he wanted a sympathetic shoulder. Naturally. She should say no. She should tell him that she was a hot chick with a lot going on and she only dated men who were emotionally available and completely into her. But the truth was that she could no more ignore someone who was hurting emotionally than a doctor could step over a person having a heart attack. At least he'd be interesting to talk to.

"All right. I'd like to have dinner with you."

He looked relieved and she realized that some of her hesitation must have shown in her face.

He hadn't asked if she was seeing anyone but then after hearing her assistant say she needed to get laid he could safely assume she was single.

The horrifying thought popped into her head that he thought she was so desperate for sex that he'd be getting more than a burger. But there was no way she was going to tell a man she hadn't gone out with yet that she wasn't planning to have sex with him.

Not only did Iris not do casual sex, his ex was too big a presence in his life. And Iris didn't do threeways.

A young woman's voice cried out, "Geoff, you made it."

Iris turned to see a woman who looked to be a couple of years younger in jeans so tight you just knew she had to lie on her back on the floor and wriggle into them. Paired with the jeans was a clingy blue top that revealed spectacular cleavage. She had layers of long blond hair and a big smile. Iris had seen her around town but never met her.

"Tara, hi." He glanced between the two women. "I'm guessing you two already know each other?"

"Actually, no. I'm Iris," she said extending her hand.

"Tara Barnes. I teach chemistry and physics at the high school. And you run that nice little bakery."

Tara had a Texas accent so it was hard to be certain but Iris got the feeling that the subtext was, I'm so smart I understand compound chemistry -- and you bake muffins for a living.

Which was probably completely unfair of her. So she said, "Yes, that's right. The Sunflower Tea and Coffee Company."

"I keep meaning to come in and have a coffee but the place is always full of my students." Subtext: you're not only dumb but you run a hangout for juvies.

She smiled. "I think I'd better go help my sister with the coffees. Since I'm an expert."

And she excused herself, heading into the kitchen.

Ever since their mother had taken up pottery and bought her own kiln, no one in the family was short of pottery, especially coffee mugs. Daphne Chance's clay creations tended to mirror her moods. When she was feeling serious, the mugs emerged from the kiln in a single color and all approximately the same size and shape.

But Daphne was rarely serious. Especially when she was potting. She sold the best of her work at local gift shops so her family tended to get the seconds. The mugs that Marguerite was pulling from the cupboard and lining up on the counter ranged from rainbow colored mugs with bulbous bottoms to curvy cups that hinted at the female body, to gnomes and fairies. "I'll make coffee," Iris said as she walked in.

"Already on."

Iris neatened up the rows of mugs. A newish collection caught her eye. "Is this supposed to be Snow White and the seven dwarfs?"

"I think so. Though Snow White looks like she melted a little bit."

"So did the little guys. Look, here's Sleazy. And Dumpy." She began to line them up. "And Dumpier."

Iris pulled a red-faced gnome over. "Is this one Bashful?"

"Or had a snootful?"

Her sister went to the fridge for the soy milk and almond milk. "Seems like you and the professor are really hitting it off."

"Teacher's got a new pet," she murmured.

Marguerite peeked into the living area where Geoff and Tara were yakking it up.

She turned back. "She's got nothing on you. Take away that long blond hair, the centerfold body and killer smile, really, she's nothing but a sharp brain."

"I am so going to beat you senseless with Dumpy."

Chapter Four

Whenever she had a birthday coming up, Iris scheduled all those annoying yearly checkups. That way she never had to remember how long it had been since her last one. Her strategy meant a flurry of appointments around the end of March each year, but then she was done.

Her eyes were still 20/20, her teeth cavity free and freshly cleaned. But, after some routine tests and an appointment with her doctor, she came out frowning.

Sunshine pricked at her eyes so she pulled sunglasses out of her bag and while she was in there, fished out her phone and made a call.

Her sister Rose didn't pick up. But then Rose almost never picked up. If her doctor sister wasn't in clinic, she was at the hospital or running a marathon or something. She'd intended to leave a message asking Rose to call her, but when she heard her sister telling her to do exactly that she heard herself saying, "I'm coming to Portland. I need a decent haircut and I want to have lunch with you. Text me a time that works for you."

And so, three days later, she left Dosana in charge with Daphne helping and drove to Portland. She'd been going to David, of David's, for five years now, every eight weeks. Usually while she was in Portland she'd do any shopping she needed to do and try to squeeze in a visit with Rose.

Iris had never seen a more stylish MD than her sister. Apart from flat shoes – though they were Prada or Chanel flats – she wore designer duds, even when they were hidden under a white lab coat. Her dark hair always looked like she'd stepped out of a salon moments ago, and her makeup was ever flawless. Iris, who had stepped out of a salon moments ago, felt like a wreck in comparison.

They hugged as they met at the restaurant door. "It's so great to see you," Rose said, squeezing her tight.

"You too."

"And lunch is my treat. You've got a birthday coming up."

"Steak and lobster sounds good," she teased. Though she didn't feel very jokey inside.

They were quickly seated at a quiet corner table which made Iris suspect that her sister was a regular here.

Rose picked up the menu immediately. She was always efficient with her time. "I'd love a glass of wine but I've got a full afternoon. You go ahead."

She shook her head. "I've got a long drive home."

They both ordered iced tea and the fish special, which was sockeye salmon flown in fresh from Alaska. That done, Rose turned her attention to her sister. Those dark eyes could focus completely; she supposed that was why Rose was such a good doctor. "What's up?" she asked.

Iris reached for a chunk of the fresh focaccia bread and pulled it apart. Then she put the pieces on her plate. "I'm sort of here for a second opinion."

"Okay." Rose waited patiently.

"I went for my annual medical checkup the other day and everything's fine. I'm not sick or anything."

"Oh, thank God. You had me worried."

"No. Sorry. No. I want your opinion on—" She blew out a breath. "Well, I had, have I guess, endometriosis."

"Okay. Not that uncommon in women in your age group who haven't given birth. It's basically uterine cells that have migrated outside the uterus. Unless it's causing a lot of pain, it's not a big deal."

"It's on my fallopian tubes. My doc said that if I want to have kids I should have them soon."

Rose paused in the act of lifting her glass to her mouth. "You want kids?" She asked the way she'd ask her sister if she wanted a dose of rabies.

She nodded.

"We grew up in a house with eleven children and you want more?"

"Crazy, I know."

"You of all people. As the oldest, I saw how Mom relied on you. I mean, you've practically been a mother for most of your life."

"I know. All that practice shouldn't go to waste, right?"

"You seriously want children."

"I do."

"Wow. I am never having kids."

"I know."

Their fish came at that moment and they took a few minutes to enjoy first bites, then Rose said, "You mentioned a second opinion."

"Well? Is she right? Should I have kids soon?"

Rose took a moment to think. "Yes, probably. Statistically your fertility takes a big drop anyway at thirty-five. If your fallopian tubes are narrowed or blocked it's going to be hard for you to get pregnant. There are procedures and new breakthroughs every day but why go there if you can avoid it?"

Normally in a restaurant she'd check out the service, be tasting the bread with an expert's discrimination, but today she was more interested in the talk than the food.

"I've always wanted kids of my own. I can't imagine my life without them."

"Are you seeing someone?"

"No. And in Hidden Falls I'm running out of options. The men are taken or they're gross or they're gone." She thought of Geoff McLeod. "Or emotionally unavailable."

"You could move."

"For a guy? Please."

Her sister's lips twitched.

"I'm thinking of doing it alone."

"Sperm bank?"

"Yeah."

"That's expensive."

"I know. I looked it up online."

"What about a friend with benefits? A baby daddy?"

Rose glanced at her watch and signaled for the waiter. She pulled out her wallet and retrieved a credit card. "I need to get back but you stay and have whatever you want."

"No. I'm done. I'll walk you back to work."

As they left the restaurant, weak sun danced off puddles from a recent rain.

"I thought of finding some guy to father the baby but it seems complicated. First, there's no one I want to sleep with (who wasn't emotionally unavailable) and second I don't want my kid going to find their dad someday and being disappointed."

Rose reached out and gave her a quick one-armed hug. "You never should have gone looking for your birth parents."

Iris in Bloom

"No. I shouldn't." Jack and Daphne Chance had always been honest that their many children had come to them in various ways, but they were adamant that every child was their son or daughter. There'd been no differentiation between natural born and adopted. Jack had come through the foster system and he was determined that no child in his home would ever feel different or less special than another. The deal was, if you wanted to know all the details you had to wait until you were sixteen.

Iris supposed it was a good policy, except that she'd not only found out she was adopted but she'd followed that up by searching out her birth parents. It had been one of the most devastating experiences of her life.

"I don't want that to happen to my kid. So I'll be honest that he or she was fathered by a gorgeous, brilliant med student who needed the money. There's no rejection in that."

The yeasty aroma of rising sweet bread dough, soon to be cinnamon buns, filled the air in the kitchen. While the dough was rising, Iris made lemon squares and kept an ear out in case Dosana became overwhelmed with a morning rush.

She loved her bakery, the chaos and the comfort of it. Serving hot beverages to get people going in the morning or to pick them up in the afternoon. She loved the pre-work crowd, always in a hurry, followed by the overtired moms who came in dragging strollers and packing bottles of milk or Tupperware boxes filled with fish-shaped crackers for the kids. She liked the old people who wandered in with the newspaper, maybe open to the crossword puzzle and settled down with all the time in the world. She loved her go cup crowd and the sit down and stay awhile crowd.

29

She sprinkled icing sugar over her fresh-from-the-oven lemon bars, their sharp-sweet scent overpowering the bread dough as she cut them into perfect squares with a large pizza wheel.

She headed out front to refill the bakery case and, since there were three people in the line, immediately put the tray down on the back counter and took over barista duties while Dosana took orders and money.

"Busy morning," she said, when the rush was over. "You should have called me."

"Didn't want you to burn anything." Dosana turned to her. "We need more staff."

"I know it seems like that now, but what if this is only a short term thing? I don't want to hire someone and not be able to keep them."

She shrugged. "I guess. In my business courses we talk about things like that."

"Let's see how it goes. If we're still as busy in a month, then I'll think about hiring someone else."

"Okay."

She slipped surgical gloves on, opened the case and rapidly refilled the lemon bars.

"Would you mind if I use the bakery for a project I'm doing for my marketing class?"

Dosana was pursuing a business degree.

"Um, I guess not." She wondered what that would involve and how much confidential information she'd have to offer.

The bell rang signaling another customer and Geoff McLeod walked in. "Let's talk about this later."

He was dressed for school in brown khakis, a cream denim shirt and tie. All he needed was a tweed jacket with leather elbow patches and a pipe to complete the cliché. And yet the look suited him. She found the rumpled intellectual look ridiculously sexy.

"Good morning," he said.

"Morning."

"Are those lemon bars?"

"One of my many specialties," she told him. "Here, try a bite." She'd cut off the edges and so she sliced him off a piece of the edge, picked it up with her gloved fingers and placed it on a square of parchment paper and handed it to him.

He popped the treat into his mouth and moaned in appreciation. "Oh, that is good."

"Want one?"

"Of course I want one. With coffee."

While she was filling his order, Dosana took the now empty tray back into the kitchen. Geoff leaned in and said, "I never got your number. So I could call you about dinner."

"Oh, right." After Tara the physically gifted physicist had monopolized him for the rest of the night of the vegan potluck, she'd wondered whether he even remembered he'd asked her for dinner.

"I was wondering about Thursday night?"

"Thursday?"

"Comes after Wednesday?" His eyes had the most wonderful way of gleaming when he was amused.

"I, yes. Sure. Thursday's good."

"Great. I'll pick you up at seven."

"Pick me up?"

"Don't people do that anymore? I'm surrounded by high school kids all day. It's hard to tell what adults do."

31

"Yes, of course. I only live a couple of streets over." And she wrote down the address for him and her phone number.

"Great. Thanks." He held up his cardboard coffee cup in a toast. "I'll see you then. Well, I'll see you every day probably when I come in for coffee."

The bell jingled like laughter when he opened it to leave, then stood back holding it open for the woman coming in. An attractive woman in her fifties with blond hair streaked with gray that they paid a fortune for in New York, jeans that showed a still hot bod and a jean jacket worn with a hand woven scarf. Iris knew the scarf was hand woven because she'd bought it for her mother for her birthday, in Daphne's favorite blues and greens. "Hello," her mother said beaming at Geoff. "It's Geoff, right?"

"Yes. Daphne, hello."

She was impressed that he remembered her mom's name since he'd only met her briefly at the vegan potluck, then realized that as a teacher he must be good at remembering names.

"I'm so glad I ran into you. I'm having a few people over on Saturday night for Iris's birthday. Why don't you come?"

She decided in that moment that she was never going to let Geoff go out that door again unless she ran ahead and checked that there was no embarrassment train steaming her way.

If he glanced back at her after her mother invited him to her birthday dinner she wouldn't have known it as she had her head in her hands. She heard him say, "I'd love to come."

"Fantastic. Come around six. You're not allergic to anything are you?"

"Not a thing."

"Wonderful. Look forward to seeing you then."

"Me, too," Geoff said.

"Bye."

She heard footsteps and waited until they stopped before lifting her head.

Her mother was still there.

"Isn't that nice that he's coming to your birthday."

"Why don't you get me a big T-shirt for my birthday that says Desperate Spinster all over it."

"Already ordered." She reached out and brushed the top of Iris's nose with her fingertips. "You've got flour or something all over your nose. It's adorable."

"This day just gets better and better."

"Oh, stop it. He's nice. I'm sure he could use a friend since he's new in town."

"You two are going to be great BFFs."

"Funny."

"What can I get you, Mom?"

"That nice jasmine green tea."

"The lemon bars are fresh out of the oven."

"Oh, I shouldn't but I am weak."

Daphne had her shoulders hunched so slightly that no one who didn't know her as well as Iris did would even notice. Because she did notice she made a pot of tea for two and asked Dosana to take over. "But call me when the timer goes off for the cinnamon buns."

She took a tray over to the table where her mom was sitting staring out the window and sat down.

"You don't need to sit with me, honey."

"Happy to get off my feet for a few."

They poured tea and she waited. Her mother sipped her tea, bit into a lemon square and complimented her on how good they were.

She waited.

"I wonder if you could talk to your father," Daphne suddenly said.

"What's he done this time?" Jack Chance was a kind and decent man. He was a loving husband and a good father. But he had some very odd ideas and whenever her mother said, "I wonder if you could speak to your father," she knew he'd come up with a doozy.

"He decided we should have a greenhouse," Daphne began.

"Okay." Somehow she knew it wasn't going to be as simple as going to the local garden shop and ordering up a greenhouse for delivery.

"He's decided to put it on the sunny side of the house."

"You mean like a lean-to?"

Daphne looked at her with the eyes of a woman who is barely holding it together. "I mean that if I hadn't hidden the sledgehammer, we'd be missing a wall in the front room by now."

"Why?" she cried. "Why does he do it?"

"He gets these ideas and they make sense to him."

"Can't you stop him?"

Her mother looked helpless. "You know what he's like. If I argue with him he tells me I have no vision. And then he acts so hurt that I end up giving in."

"How am I going to stop him?"

"If you can get him focused on a different project he'll have time to realize that we don't need a greenhouse in the front room."

34

"Focus on what?"

"Well, he's very good at dry walling and flooring. I was thinking maybe you could tell him you really need your attic done. Tell him you need a studio or something."

"A home office." Strangely, she'd been thinking about finishing the attic.

"Perfect." Daphne looked puzzled. "Except you already have a home office in your spare bedroom."

She took a fortifying sip of green tea. She supposed this was as good a moment as any to share her plan. "I'm thinking of turning the spare bedroom into a nursery."

Daphne was rarely shocked. After years of Jack's home handyman projects and the antics of eleven kids, she was pretty much immune. But Iris had the dubious satisfaction of knowing she'd shocked her mother speechless.

After a moment, Daphne said, "How can you be pregnant? You haven't had a date in months."

"Ouch. And I'm not pregnant. Yet." The bell rang and she heard Dosana greet someone. She leaned forward. "I'm thinking of having a baby."

"On your own?"

She nodded.

After a second her mother smiled at her. "You know I support you in anything you choose to do. If you've thought it through carefully and you're sure this is what you want then I'll do anything I can to be there for you. And my first grandchild."

She reached over and grasped her mother's hand. "Thanks, Mom." She glanced at the clock. "Okay, keep Dad busy and the sledgehammer hidden and I'll be over this afternoon."

"Bless you, Honey. You know he listens to you."

Which pretty much told her how desperate her mother was feeling.

Chapter Five

Geoff finished his school day having discovered already that Iris Chance had been right. The students had ganged up on the newbie teacher and tried to get King Lear off the curriculum. And, he'd been right that Rosalind was the first one to pull out the old, "How is a Shakespeare play relevant to me? I'm going to be a firefighter/nurse/chemical engineer/realtor/serial killer/ argument that kids in school had been using since probably Shakespeare's time.

And he countered with the same argument he imagined every high school English teacher had dusted off since that poor chap got picked on at Stratford-upon-Avon High. "The power struggle between the younger generation and the older is timeless and always relevant."

Of thirty-two students in his class, about twenty pairs of eyes stared at him balefully. The other dozen sets of eyes were staring at the ground, the ceiling, the clock, at some hopeless love interest across the aisle or sneakily trying to check the forbidden cell phone.

"King Lear is as current as the Kardashians."

That stirred a flicker of interest and got a few more pairs of eyes on him. "In fact, that will be an essay question you can choose so you can prove to yourselves that Lear is relevant. Have Act One1 read by Thursday."

Groans met him along with the thump of books hitting bags, but then the bell rang and both he and Shakespeare were forgotten as the kids poured out into the halls like a river overflowing its banks.

He packed up and headed out. The afternoon was sunny and he needed to stretch his legs. He'd do his grading in the evening when the daylight was gone.

He drove slowly home thinking that this change wasn't one he'd wanted or asked for but he was going to be okay.

He had a feeling he was going to settle into the school fine. He liked his colleagues, the kids were pretty much like teenagers everywhere. The country was pretty and he'd met an interesting woman.

Not bad for a guy who'd had his life turned upside down only two months ago.

Not bad at all.

Feeling better than he'd felt in weeks, he drove to his new apartment, thinking that he really needed to finish unpacking. Later. He changed into running gear. He drank water before he left and as he did so he flipped on his laptop to check his email.

Brianna, his wife of six years, soon to be ex-wife had emailed him. The header was Our Life Together. He clicked open the email wondering if she was asking him to come back. After the abrupt and brutal way she'd ended their marriage – with a text message, as though she were cancelling a date – he wondered if she were having second thoughts.

Geoff, After the way you verbally attacked me the last time we saw each other I no longer feel safe around you. If you want anything out of the house let me know so I can arrange not to be here.

Geoff didn't think of himself as a man who got angry very often. He liked to think of himself as pretty easy going. He might be stubborn at times -- but the kind of man his own wife wouldn't feel safe with? The unfairness of it all bubbled up in him until he felt as though his eyeballs were vibrating with bitterness.

He sat down and began hammering out a furious reply when it suddenly hit him. She was playing him. He didn't know why or how but the stupidest thing he could do right now was to answer her in writing.

He pushed away from the desk, grabbed the keys to his apartment and ran out the door. He pounded down the apartment stairs, hit the street and started running. Instinctively, he headed away from town to the country roads. He started out going way too fast until he was wheezing air into his parched lungs. He slowed, getting off the main road and onto the small country lanes where traffic was rare.

He found a rhythm and tried to pound the anger at Brianna's unfair accusation out into the gravel. Inside his head he ranted, he swore, he told his ex what he thought of her.

He didn't realize how much of a pent up mad he had going on until he finally slowed his steps, his shirt drenched with sweat and his muscles aching. Time to turn around and head for home.

He had no idea how long he'd been running. Based on the ache in his calves it had been a while. As he turned, he experienced the sinking feeling that he didn't know which way was home.

All around him were fields that he barely remembered passing, lanes and roads criss-crossed. There wasn't so much as a road sign.

He had run himself into the middle of nowhere.

Somewhere there must be a house or a major road or something, he thought as he began to trudge, wishing he'd at least brought his cell phone so he had a GPS and could, if absolutely desperate, call for help.

Instead, he had the setting sun to guide him. Sun sets in the west. He decided to follow it knowing he'd have to start running again soon simply to stay warm.

The late March weather was spring-like. While the sun had been out there'd been some warmth but as it faded he felt the crispness in the air.

He had a momentary image of him dying out here of hypothermia. And wouldn't that be humiliating? He trudged on adding getting him lost to the list of sins for which he blamed Brianna.

Iris left her parents' house, refusing an offer to stay for dinner. She liked to move ahead on a project once she'd decided on a course and tonight she was going to start shopping for a baby daddy.

She saw a lone jogger up ahead and as she drew near, to her astonishment, he turned around and stuck out a thumb. Her headlights told her two things. First, the guy out jogging was Geoff McLeod and second, he'd overdone the workout. She pulled to a stop and got out. "Geoff? Are you okay?"

"Iris. Good to see you." He sounded all fake casual but she could see he was drenched in sweat and, since the sunset had brought colder air, he was shivering. He wasn't carrying water so she flipped her trunk and grabbed one of the bottles she always carried for emergencies. "Here."

"Water. Thanks." He opened the top and drank deeply. Then he looked at her. "I got lost."

"So I see. Get in. I'll drive you home."

He looked down at himself and pulled the shirt away from his body. She couldn't help but notice some seriously nice pecs and abs where the shirt had shrink wrapped to his skin. "I'm soaked."

Back to the open trunk. "My workout gear's in the back." She unzipped the duffel that always rode with her in case she was overcome with an urge to hit the gym. There was a towel folded neatly at the bottom. "Here you go."

"Thanks." He mopped his face. Then opened the passenger door and laid the towel on the seat before getting in.

She banged the trunk shut and got back behind the wheel. Only by force of will did she resist the urge to scold him for running out without his cell phone or water or the most basic survival essentials. She was not his mother and he was a grown man who could figure out for himself how foolish he'd been.

"You must think I'm a fool," he said and she wondered if he could read minds.

"I'm glad I came along when I did."

He turned his head and his eyes glittered in the dim light. "Me, too."

"So, where's home?"

He gave her the address and since she wasn't lost, she was able to drive straight there. "You ran a long way," she said as they drew closer to town.

"I got an email from my wife." His tone was bitter. "Soon to be ex-wife," he corrected himself. "I lost my mind for long enough to get totally disoriented. And I ran way farther than I intended to." She heard clipped annoyance but she thought it was directed at himself.

When they pulled up in front of an older walk-up, he said, "Thanks. You saved my butt out there."

"You're welcome."

He reached for the door handle then turned back to her. "Could I interest you in pizza and a beer?"

She'd planned to spend the evening researching sperm banks, but she also knew that Geoff did not want to be alone tonight.

She didn't imagine they were going to run out of sperm at the sperm bank if she waited until tomorrow.

"Do you have wine?"

"I do."

"You have a deal." So, instead of dropping him off, she parked and followed him inside and up the stairs.

He opened the door with his key and stood back to let her go first. There were moving boxes stacked like kids' blocks. Empty bookshelves and furniture so new the tags were hanging off them.

"It's a mess," he said. "Sorry. I'm still moving in."

He walked straight to the sink in the galley kitchen and poured himself a huge glass of water and gulped it back, one hand holding onto the edge of the counter.

He refilled the glass and turned to her. "You probably know the best pizza place. Tell me there is a place that delivers."

"Of course there is. Alfredo's. Okay if I use your computer to search the number?"

"Yeah. Oh, wait." He scooted ahead of her and hit a button. The swirling blue dots of his screensaver disappeared and up came an email. He hit delete and then put the email file away. "Okay, there you go. Order whatever you want. I'll go shower."

He halted mid way to the door she assumed led to the bathroom. "Wine." And headed once more to the kitchen. "Red or white?"

She wrinkled her nose. "What goes with pizza? Red?"

"Everything goes with pizza." He opened a cupboard and she saw neatly stacked bottles in a wine rack. "I stopped at Napa on my way here. Got a case of this stuff. It's fantastic."

He opened a bottle, poured her a glass and then said, "Okay, shower. Make yourself at home."

She found Alfredo's number and ordered an extra large with everything.

That done, she settled on a couch so new that he hadn't yet taken off the plastic on the armrests.

She did that. And then walked over to the empty bookshelves. Normally she loved to browse other people's books but his were all boxed up. Five or six boxes hunched beside two empty bookshelves.

Each box had Books written in black felt pen. Seeing an easy way to help him get rid of a couple of boxes, she ripped packing tape off the first book box. General human psychology books with specific volumes of Freud and Jung. She placed them in the bottom shelf feeling that he could always rearrange the books later if he didn't like her system. The next layer of books made her pause. Human sexuality seemed to be the theme. Some volumes on teenage sexuality and talking to teens about sex. Okay. Then she came across a big book on tantric sex. And another. And yet a third.

She settled on the hardwood floor, her back against the new couch, reached for her wine and opened the most interesting looking book.

Chapter Six

Geoff let the hot water pound down on him hoping he could head off the stiff muscles he suspected he'd earned. What the hell had he been thinking? Truth was he hadn't been thinking at all. Allowing a mad on to drive him to run so far he was not only exhausted and dehydrated but lost?

That adventure was right up there with the most bone-headed moves of his life. He was grateful that Iris had been driving by but somehow that made it worse. He wished he'd been rescued by a farmer who rarely went into town and didn't talk much when he did. Not an attractive woman whose coffee shop was the gossip hub of Hidden Falls.

He scrubbed himself clean, shampooed and rapidly shaved and brushed his teeth. He felt that if he was inviting a woman into his home, even for an impromptu pizza, the least he could do was spruce up.

He reached for his robe and discovered it wasn't on the hook behind the door where he always kept it because this bathroom door didn't have a hook and he hadn't got around to putting one up. Which meant his robe was in his bedroom. Which meant he was going to have to walk past Iris in a towel.

He wrapped the largest towel he could find, a navy blue bath sheet, around his waist, tying it securely. Then he walked out into the living area wondering who the hell designed a layout where the bathroom was all the way across the living room from the bedroom.

She glanced up when he emerged and he saw her eyes widen slightly as she took in his half naked state. "I'll just, ah, go get dressed," he said as he started to walk toward his bedroom. A flash of – something – arced between them. Awareness? Connection? Then he realized she was starting to unpack boxes, seemed to have got caught up in reading one of the books, which was exactly the kind of thing he would do. He walked as quickly and in as dignified manner as a man, naked but for a towel, can walk. He ducked into his bedroom and quickly threw on well-worn jeans and an athletics shirt from his last school.

When he emerged she was still engrossed in the book. She sipped her wine and barely seemed to notice him as he drew closer. Curious, he leaned in to see what had caught her attention. Slow Sex. He investigated the contents of the box she'd opened and the books she'd shelved. Sex and psychology -- and half the psych books were about sex.

She must think he was a pervert.

"You know, I have boxes of books all about philosophy, most of the classics and an entire box devoted to horror novels."

She glanced up. "This is fascinating. All I've ever known abut tantric sex is that Sting and his wife go at it for something like thirty-six hours at a time." She rested the book on her knees. "I bet that's not even true. I hope I like sex as much as the next girl, but thirty-six hours?" She sipped wine. "Did you ever—" Then she shook her head. "Sorry. Engaged mouth before brain. I do that sometimes."

He felt the knot that had twisted his guts since he'd read that email start to ease. "Not thirty-six hours. No. But there's something to be said for taking your time."

She nodded. "This should be required reading for every man." Then, "I can't believe I did it again." She snapped the book shut. "It's this book getting me into trouble."

If anyone had asked him three months ago if he'd be sitting in an apartment which he alone occupied discussing tantric sex with a pretty woman who was not his wife, he'd have said they were crazy. Now he wondered if he was the crazy one being married to someone he obviously hadn't known at all.

He poured himself a glass of wine, brought the bottle over and topped up her glass.

"I've got music, somewhere." He glanced around, knowing he had one of those apartment sized sound systems in one of the boxes. Also an iPod full of tunes. Somewhere.

"Maybe if I help you unpack a few of these boxes we'll find it."

"Or some other remnant of my past sex life."

She grinned at him. "Come on. You can tell me which boxes to avoid. We could at least get the book cases filled."

"You don't have to help me unpack. You already saved my life tonight."

"That might be a slight exaggeration. But I'm glad I came along when I did."

"Me, too."

"Okay, you heft this heavy one and you can tell me if you have a particular system for books."

"Sounds good to me." He did have a sort of system but he figured he could always rearrange things when she was gone.

By the time the pizza arrived, they were halfway through the second box. They'd have finished all the books except that she kept stopping to say, "Oh, I love Sherlock Holmes," or "this book changed my life."

She came across an Alice Munro book of short stories and held it to her breast like she was giving an old friend a hug. "Alice Munro is the most brilliant short story writer. I was so happy when she won the Nobel Prize." She placed the book, Progress of Love, carefully on the shelf. "I had a copy of this but I lent it to someone and never got it back."

"I hate it when that happens." Then he glanced over at her. "Do you want to borrow this one?"

"God, no. I don't want to forget to give it back and one day you tell the story about me forgetting to give a treasured book back to you."

When the pizza arrived he collected it, generously tipping the kid – who he thought might be a student at Jefferson High, though not in any of his classes.

He carried the box to the kitchen and lifted the lid. "What kind of pizza is this?" It was so loaded it was hard to tell.

"I wasn't sure what you like so I got everything."

"Excellent choice." He pulled his new plates from the cupboard and carried everything over to the couch and put it on the low table he'd bought.

He offered her the box and watched her take a piece of pizza, dragging it straight to her mouth and biting off the end.

He grabbed his own slice and discovered that she'd told the truth. It was really good pizza. He didn't realize how hungry he'd been. They ate the better part of a piece each, too blissed out by all the cheese and sauce and every possible topping, to talk. She was easy company, restful.

Until she glanced over at him and said, "Do you want to talk about it?"

He swallowed and suddenly the pizza was all crust.

"You mean the email?"

"I mean whatever got you racing twelve miles to the middle of nowhere."

He did want to talk about it and he didn't. Maybe simply talking the pain through would help him process. So, he said, "I was married for six years. I thought it was a pretty good marriage. Not maybe the greatest love story of all time, but who gets that? I don't know. You go to work, you pay your mortgage, you live your life. Is it really supposed to be a constant never-ending honeymoon?"

"Is that what she expected?"

He tried to think about whether what he was saying was even true. "I don't know." He stared at the dark red liquid in the bowl of the wine glass. "We never even talked about what was wrong. I was out of town for a school trip and on my way home I got a text from her saying she'd moved out. Our marriage was over. I was on a yellow school bus with a bunch of high school kids and she ended our marriage."

He looked over at Iris and found her quietly watching him, felt her sympathy. "She ended a six year marriage with a text message?"

"Yeah."

"That is harsh."

"It was like having a car accident or getting shot or something. One minute you're going along and your life is on a path you can see ahead for miles. And in an instant the path's not there anymore. It's a cliff and you're going over it and there's nothing you can do."

"You didn't have any clue at all?"

He winced. "I know. It makes me sound like I was completely out of touch with my own wife. My own marriage." He shifted back feeling the weight of his own discomfort. "Maybe I was and didn't even know it."

"And today?"

"I really think I tried to be an adult about the break up. She didn't want to be married anymore. She'd moved out. I knew I couldn't stay in that town anymore and risk bumping into her or see her dating guys I probably knew. It was too crazy. So I took this job and moved. And today I got an email basically saying she doesn't trust me and I verbally attacked her. I completely lost it."

He shook his head.

"Did you verbally attack her?"

"There were some heated words when I tried to figure out what was going on and she wouldn't even talk to me. But I didn't call her names or anything. No."

"Did you reply to her email?"

"Started to but it was like the unfairness of it all was choking me. I had to get out and run off some of the frustration. I left it half written."

"Okay, I know you are hurting and you're mad. I have no idea what's going on obviously but you've got to be strategic. From now on, you have to make an unbreakable deal with yourself that you let at least four hours go by before you respond to any email from your wife or about her."

Even in his black mood he had to smile. "Four hours? Is that the rule?"

"It's my rule. And it's unbreakable. You will save yourself a world of pain."

"Experience talking?"

"Common sense. And watching other people do stupid things because they were angry and in pain."

"You're right. I can't believe I almost sent off something filled with rage. Stupid."

"Rage tends to make people stupid."

He reached out with his bare foot and nudged her crossed ankles on the table. "Where did you learn to be so smart?"

"Oldest girl? Ten brothers and sisters? There is nothing you can teach me about drama. Or stupidity."

"I'd have said the same for me having taught high school for so long. Truth is, I'm shocked this happened to me."

He saw her hesitate, choose her words carefully, then their gazes met and she said, "Could she have met someone else?"

"It was my first thought. She denied it, blew up at me for suggesting it, and none of my friends have said anything." He shrugged. "I don't know."

"But you have your suspicions?" She must have read it in his tone.

"Yeah. I do. Why else would she break up so fast without so much as a conversation, a few counseling sessions, something."

She reached out. Put her hand on his. "I'm sorry."

He turned his hand palm-up, clasped hers. "Thanks."

The warmth of the connection that sprang between them from their clasped hands shocked him. He glanced up and found her looking startled.

She eased her hand slowly away. "I should get back. I've got an early start in the morning." She made a production of closing the pizza box. "I have to bake muffins."

"I definitely want you fresh tomorrow since I will be coming in for one of those muffins."

She rose. "Thanks for dinner."

He followed her to the door and opened it for her. "Thanks for hanging out with me tonight."

"Hope I helped a little."

"More than you know," and he leaned forward and kissed her cheek. She smelled so good, as though all the spices and sweet ingredients she used in her cooking, plus a hint of the coffee she spent her days dispensing had somehow become part of her. The skin of her cheek was silky against his lips. He wondered what would happen if he took the kiss to her mouth, was thinking about it when she pulled away.

"See you tomorrow," she said, and was gone so fast she left a jet stream.

Interesting.

Chapter Seven

The espresso machine steamed and hissed its good morning greeting, the first batch of muffins was baked, the cinnamon rolls minutes away from done. All her familiar routines settled Iris as she prepared to open Sunflower the next morning.

Dosana arrived, a new streak of cranberry slicing her jet black hair so she looked, at first glance, like the victim of a hatchet attack.

"What do you think?" she asked, seeing Iris stare.

"It looks very -- red." What could she say? Suggesting to an employee that her new hairstyle looked like the result of a botched murder attempt was not going to be conducive to harmonious owner/staff relations.

"Thanks. I needed a change. I've got papers due and exams coming up. So I dyed my hair. Figured if I'm going to procrastinate, I should do something fun that won't get me hung over."

Dosana was in her final year of her business degree. Since she was entirely self-funded she had to juggle school and her nearly full time hours at Sunflower. Iris planned the schedule around her busiest times and it worked for both of them. She'd be sorry to see Dosana go when she graduated and went on to greater things.

"I still want to make this bakery my case study for graduation. What do you think?"

"Will I have to give away all my secrets?"

Dosana looked amused. "You think a bunch of college kids care about your recipe for morning glory muffins?"

"I meant my finances smart ass."

"I think we can work in general terms so you only divulge what you're comfortable with." She moved in for the sales pitch. "And, you know, in return you're going to get advice from business pros who help mentor students."

"I could definitely use some advice." She shrugged. "Sure. Why not?"

Dosana hugged her. "That's fantastic. Thanks. I'll email you with everything I need. Speaking of which, I think we're short on those organic brown sugar packets."

"Really? Check the next delivery. It should be on my computer."

Dosana returned in a second carrying Iris's laptop with her. "What is this?"

"Oh, right. That." She'd forgotten to log out of the sperm bank website. Damn. She tried to act completely casual. "I've been playing with the idea of maybe having a baby."

"Alone?" Why did she make it sound so pathetic? A decade from now Dosana might find out that being a single business owner in a small town meant there was a pretty small pool of eligible men.

"Like I said, I'm only toying with the idea."

"Shopping for a baby daddy," she said in a teasing tone.

"Don't tell anyone. Okay?"

Dosana was checking out the likely candidates on the website, her nose ring winking every time she shook her head. Then she glanced up. "What about that cute English teacher? Mr. McLeod? He's hot, he's smart and you get the feeling he knows his way around the female body if you know what I mean."

She knew exactly what Dosana meant. "He's complicated."

"All the interesting ones are."

"Still married."

"Getting a divorce."

She raised her brows. "How do you know?"

"Please. Sunflower is gossip central."

"How come I haven't heard anyone gossiping about Geoff and his divorce?"

Dosana turned to busy herself with returning the computer to the back room.

And then she got it. She hadn't heard because she was part of the gossip mill rumors.

Her suspicion was confirmed when Dosana returned. "What are you wearing on your date with him on Thursday?"

"How do you know I have a date with him Thursday?"

"Everyone knows you have a date with him Thursday."

She was still thinking about that when the bell rang and Geoff himself walked in. He wore his usual teacher uniform, only this time he wore jeans with a shirt and skinny tie. She thought he was limping slightly and trying not to let it show so she decided not to mention the impromptu half marathon he'd completed yesterday.

"Hi," he said, all sexy voiced and still married to another woman.

"Hi." She tried to sound bright, and really, really busy even though he was the first customer and her café was empty.

He stood in front of her counter and there was a moment of silence with a lot of unspoken packed into it. Finally, she said, "You've been coming here long enough that I can ask

54

you if you want the usual?" she asked. "Americano and a muffin."

"Sure."

"Coming right up."

"About Thursday, how do you feel about driving an hour or so? I've been asking around about restaurants and it seems like—"

"We already had dinner. Last night."

"That was pizza delivery after you saved my life and gave me a ride home. Thursday, if you'll recall, is a date."

She let the hiss of the espresso machine give her a second to put her thoughts straight, then said, "About Thursday, I'm not sure it's a good idea."

"Is it because I got lost? Honestly, I have a good sense of direction normally."

She turned to him. Looked into those disappointed blue eyes. "It's because you're still married. And I don't want to get involved with someone who is still so wrapped up in another woman that an email sends him running himself half to death."

She passed him his coffee, got the tongs and flipped a muffin expertly into a bag.

"I, I don't know what to say. I like you."

"I like you, too."

The jingle of bells announced another customer.

"Then can't we—"

"Hi Mr. McLeod." A chorus of young female voices had him turning his head. The girls' swim team, between early morning practice and school, had stopped in for sustenance. Most of the six who'd cruised inside—more like one organism than six individual people—still sported wet hair and glowed with athleticism.

"Morning girls."

He picked up his coffee and his bag, glanced with pent up frustration at Iris, said, "Thanks," and headed out.

The door barely shut behind him when one of the girls said, "He's so dreamy."

"I know, right? Ms. Barnes and him are totally going to fall in love."

Iris realized that even in a small town there were different gossip centers. At Jefferson High they didn't seem to know that she and the English teacher were supposed to go out Thursday night.

Except that she'd blown him off, leaving the way totally clear for Ms. Barnes.

"Red hair with bad eyes and a Harvard education or altogether better looking with a lower IQ but perfect eyesight?" Iris asked Marguerite as they sat together in front of her computer.

"Is there a way to get a kid that looks more like you?" Marguerite asked.

"Are you kidding me? You can look at donors' childhood photos, adult photos, you can try and get someone who looks similar to you or – and this is probably my favorite trick – you can pick a donor who looks like a celebrity."

"You have got to be kidding me."

"Nope."

"So the future could see lots of pint sized Pitts and jacked up Jackmans? Some petite Paltrows and knee high Hathaways." Marguerite was cracking herself up. "Oh, I have to stop. Who wants a designer kid?"

"I want a healthy one. That's all."

Marguerite kept scrolling through photos.

"Online dating has nothing on shopping for a baby daddy."

"Except that a bad online date lasts as long as it takes to gulp down a coffee. Choose the wrong sperm donor and I'm stuck with my mistake for life."

"Worse, your poor as yet unconceived child is stuck with bad choice DNA."

"So not helpful."

She slumped in the chair in her home office that would soon be a nursery if all went according to plan. "Do you think I'm making a terrible mistake?"

Marguerite leaned back too. Took a sip of herbal tea from the lumpy purple mug that sort of resembled the botanical Iris. Iris had a set of six of them, some more successful than others. "I honestly don't know what I think. I'm a couple of years younger than you and I don't have issues that would get in the way of conceiving." She pushed a hand through her hair. "I'm still far more concerned with not getting pregnant than with trying to. But it's your body, your life. You should do whatever makes you happy." She grinned. "And I'll be a killer aunt."

"Mom would never say anything but I feel like they believe I should take in a stray, like they always did." She sighed. "Like I am."

"Hey. Mom had kids of her own, too. And their path isn't your path."

"Thanks, Sis."

They continued baby daddy shopping, putting the likeliest candidates in a favorites file.

Harvard didn't make the cut. The better looking guy with perfect eyes and a lower IQ did.

"You know what's weird?"

"What?"

"I'm learning things about myself from the way I choose a potential donor."

Marguerite nodded. "Yeah, like you prize looks over smarts. But not completely. You want a good looking kid with a chance at a normal childhood."

"Am I a very shallow woman?"

"At least you're not trying to create a freak with a gigantic IQ. And thank God you're not going for a Dunst doppelganger, a jolie Jolie," she said in her perfect French accent, "A pebble off the Rock, a—"

Luckily she was spared any more of Marguerite's hilarity when her cell phone rang. Call display told her it was Geoff McLeod calling. Looks and brains, she thought as she picked up.

"Hi, Iris, it's Geoff."

"I know, I have call display."

"And still you picked up. My day's improving." Maybe it was that slightly sleepy tone he always had, as though he was just getting out of bed, or thinking of getting into it. His voice was one of the most attractive things about him.

"I didn't mean to offend you this morning."

"You blew me off on a date I've been looking forward to all week."

She immediately felt guilty. She knew from the self-help books that littered her bookshelf the way tantric sex books littered Geoff's, that the guilt response was part of her people pleasing issues. She needed to be honest and not back down. "I don't think you're ready."

She could hear the low rumble of the TV in the background. "We got interrupted so fast you didn't even give me the 'let's be friends' speech." There was a teasing note but also the honest message of a man who needs a friend.

Did she want to be his friend? His volunteer therapist and the person who made him feel better about his break-up?

She sort of thought she did.

"Of course we can be friends."

"Great. Friends do dinner, right?"

She couldn't help but laugh. "You asked me on a date."

"And now I'm amending the invitation to friends."

"If we go as friends, we split the bill."

He sighed. "You're going to be a pain in the ass friend, aren't you?"

"Probably."

"So? Can we still go out Thursday?"

She debated with herself then went with the truth. Even though Marguerite was eavesdropping on every word without even pretending she wasn't. "My problem is I find you attractive. If we go for dinner then I might forget we're only friends."

"Okay." He forestalled her before she could turn him down for dinner yet again. "How about this. Friends help each other, right?"

"Sure. Of course."

"I bought some furniture from a big box Swedish place. I need help putting it together."

"You're asking me to build furniture?"

"No. I'm asking you to have dinner with me, but if you don't want dinner, then I'm offering you an alternative, a mentally and physically stimulating evening of building furniture. And, as an enticement, there will be dinner."

"More pizza?"

"I heard the Thai place is good. I could get take-out."

When she got off the phone, Marguerite widened her eyes. Since she'd already explained to her sister why she'd blown him off for Thursday, she had to explain the new relationship.

"So, you're going to spend Thursday evening with the professor anyway?"

"As a friend. Besides, he's getting Thai. You know how much I love Thai food."

Chapter Eight

So what did you wear to a date that had turned into a friends-only non-date? A furniture building non-date? After work Iris was overcome with a sudden compulsion to hit the gym. An hour of treadmill, weights and stretching reminded her that she needed to do this a whole lot more often.

She came home, showered and decided eventually on jeans and a plain white T-shirt. Casual. Then she spent longer than usual on her makeup and wore her favorite earrings.

Friends, she thought as she picked up the box she'd prepared earlier with two lemon bars alongside two of her wicked brownies. Her take-out bakery boxes had the Sunflower logo stamped on the top.

When she knocked on his door she really wondered what she was doing. He opened and she was momentarily surprised to see him out of his teacher uniform. He had on a gray athletic T with a hole in the shoulder and jeans that hung low on his hips. His feet were bare.

"Hi," he said.

"Hi." She offered the box and he took it, giving her a hopeful look. "Is this what I'm hoping it is?"

"If you're hoping Lady Gaga's going to jump out and sing Bad Romance then no. If you're hoping for wicked brownies and lemon bars, then yes."

"Lady Gaga is nothing compared to your lemon bars."

"You're buttering me up in hopes I know how to use an Allen wrench," she said as she walked inside. He'd made some progress, she noted since she was last here. Fewer boxes skulked in corners needing unpacking and the place looked more lived in.

"Do you?"

"I always get my dad to put together my stuff."

He shut the door behind her and she looked around. "You have a cat?"

He glanced at the calico curled up in the corner of the couch. "I have a new buddy who knows how to climb in my window and doesn't like to be alone."

"Oh, he's so cute." She walked over to where two wide green eyes assessed her. Probably with jealousy. "What's his name? Her name?"

"I have no idea. I call it Cat." He turned to her. "You're not allergic or anything, are you?"

"No. I like cats." She scratched this one on the head and was immediately rewarded by throaty purring. "Where is the construction project?"

"Bedroom."

"Oh." Okay, they were friends. This wasn't weird. And they had a chaperone. She walked to the open bedroom door and peeked in, noticed that he'd got as far as opening a box and laying out an enormous number of pieces. A bag of screws and strange colorful plastic things and the dreaded Allen wrench lay beside the pieces. A second unopened box was propped against the white wall.

"They're going to be night tables. I didn't know there'd be so many pieces."

"How hard can it be? We're two intelligent, creative people."

"Positive thinking. I like that."

She went straight for the directions assuming he, being a man, wouldn't bother with them.

She flipped through once. Twice. Flopped to the hardwood floor with her back leaning against the bed. "Where are the words?"

He shook his head. "No words. Pictures."

"I don't even know what these diagrams mean."

"Very visual people, the Swedes."

"Are you visual?"

"Words all the way."

She flipped through the diabolical picture reel one more time. "We are so screwed."

"Maybe wine will help," he offered.

"It can't hurt."

He got out another bottle of the wine he'd bought in Napa, uncorked it and poured two glasses. "This should take care of the squiggles," he said with great optimism.

While they struggled through the wordless diagrams and screwed pieces to other pieces, she said, "How's it going with the ex?"

"You don't want to hear this."

She nearly dropped the silver screw thing that she was pushing into a predrilled hole. She couldn't remember the last time someone resisted the urge to share their problems with her when invited to do so. "Sure I do. It's like a TV show where I was left on a cliffhanger."

"Well, the main character in your show fell off that cliff."

His voice sounded clipped, business like. That had to be bad. "I was afraid of that. What happened?"

"I called my buddy the lawyer and asked him to represent me in the divorce. We've been friends for years, we used to run together. We've socialized, my wife and I and his girlfriend and him. We even went on a ski trip one Christmas."

"Uh-huh?" She stopped screwing her silver screw into its pre-drilled hole so she could give him her full attention.

"He said he was sorry but he couldn't take my case. For personal reasons."

"Oh, he's not." But of course she knew he was. Oldest crime in the book.

"Screwing my wife? Oh, yes he is."

"How can people be so awful? So disloyal? Your wife and your best friend? The two people on earth you should most be able to trust."

"I don't know. But I found another lawyer. A woman who is happily married. She'll represent me in my divorce."

He pushed pieces together and made a drawer. "And the sooner I'm free the better."

Daphne Chance loved to get as many of her offspring under her roof at the same time as possible as often as practical. Birthdays and major holidays were good bets that she'd be entertaining a hefty portion of her brood under her roof, at least for a few hours.

Since Iris knew this, she let her mother invite whoever she wanted to the birthday party, figuring that she'd already done her embarrassing worst by inviting Geoff.

To her delight, Iris got an email from her older brother, Evan. He and his fiancée Caitlyn were driving the two hundred miles to come for her party and spending the weekend with Daphne and Jack.

After the horror story Evan had almost married, the Chance family had heaved a collective sigh when they met the woman who'd stolen his heart for good. Caitlyn Sorenson was not the woman any of them could have imagined Evan with. She'd chosen to run a country medical practice in a small town. To everyone's surprise, Evan had followed her lead and given up his huge time and soul-sucking corporate law practice to join with a single partner in a two-person law firm.

And yet when you saw them together it was obvious that Caitlyn was exactly right for him. Since he'd settled with her, Evan had never appeared happier.

Since Daphne had kept on inviting people she'd gone way past the number that could fit around her huge dining table so the dinner would be buffet style. "I'm always intimidated cooking for you," Daphne said as she went over the menu one more time.

"Mom, I love your food. It's nice for me to have a break from cooking."

"And you want your favorite cake for dessert?"

"It wouldn't feel like my birthday without your strawberry shortcake."

"Okay." It was true, too. Daphne's strawberry shortcake was as much a part of celebrating her birthday as was the dinner gathering.

On the day of her party she wore her favorite dress. It was a midnight blue, and very flattering to her figure. Maybe she was dressing up a little more than she usually did but it was her birthday. Of course she should look her best. She wore it with a Lapis lazuli and amethyst pendant and her dangly amethyst earrings. She took the time to do her makeup properly and even spent an unheard of half-hour on her hair.

While she was doing that, she took Happy Birthday calls from her friends and the sibs who couldn't make it. She had a wall of greetings on her Facebook page and her email box was satisfyingly full of messages.

When she arrived at the house she'd grown up in it was full of noise. Six of the Chance kids were here and there was the usual boisterous catching up to do.

"Here she is, here's the birthday girl," Jack announced, getting up and pulling her in for a hug. "My beautiful girl. Look at you all grown up."

He made her sound like she was eighteen instead of thirty-three. She kissed his cheek and whispered, "Has it been very bad today?"

"Not too bad," he whispered back, his eyes twinkling. "She only had me go into town three times for things she forgot."

There was no time for more as her sibs dragged her into the large living area. Nothing would ever make this room elegant. Architectural Digest would never knock on the door and beg for a photo shoot, but with all the newspapers and books and half-finished knitting projects put away, the old furniture polished and flowers everywhere, it looked as good as it ever would. In honor of her birthday, her mother had vases of irises spiking purples everywhere. However, since Iris's favorite flower was, in fact, the sunflower, the huge happy heads grinned at the purple spikes as though knowing they'd be grinning their happy heads off long after the irises had wilted and died.

As people began to arrive the room filled with conversation and laughter. This, she thought, was why she'd never left Hidden Falls. There were friends here she'd known since she was in elementary school and high school, others she'd worked with over the years.

Iris in Bloom

Dosana was here in a black leather skirt and boots, her sleeveless gray shirt showing off her shoulder tattoo.

Lucky, the family rescue mutt, a golden lab who was convinced she was the twelfth child of the family, got into the swing of the party by dropping her disgusting gooey tennis ball in the laps of anyone foolish to sit with their knees at her head height. Then she backed up a step and stood, staring fixedly at the ball, her tail swinging slowly back and forth.

The odd foolish person who didn't know her very well would throw the ball a few feet. This was a mistake as it meant that Lucky would never, ever, stop retrieving the ball and plopping it back into their lap until one of them died of old age or a family member came by and put an end to the game.

As Iris watched Cooper, her youngest brother, take the ball from Scott Beatty's lap and head outside, Lucky in hot pursuit, Evan came and sat beside her. The two doctors, Caitlyn and Rose, were deep in conversation. Not about medicine, about shoes. They made a striking pair, both gorgeous, Rose dark and Caitlyn fair, and both deeply girly.

"You'd never know those two were trained medical professionals," her big brother said, shaking his head at the women as he settled back in the chintz chair beside hers.

"Please don't expect support from me on that subject." She extended her own feet to show him. "For what these cost? I could have bought a new lawnmower and it would have been more practical. But I love my shoes."

"Happy Birthday, kid," he said. Pulling her in for a hug.

"Thanks. I'm so glad you came. And brought Caitlyn. We all love her. When I think of that lemon Popsicle you almost married…?"

67

He shuddered. "Don't remind me."

"You look happy," she said. And he did. "Being a small town lawyer suits you."

"So far. It's a different life than I ever imagined for myself."

"I think this is better."

He laughed. Then glanced at his almost wife. "I think so too."

"No wedding jitters?"

"Not a one. My only fear is that she'll realize she's making a huge mistake and dump my ass before I've got her tied down."

She chuckled. Anyone could see these two were as deeply in love as Daphne and Jack, though hopefully not so embarrassing as to fondle each other in front of company as she could see her parents doing in the dining room doorway.

Geoff could hear the noise of talk and laughter as he stepped up to the door and rang the bell. It was opened to him by Daphne who wore a big smile and smudged lipstick. She hugged him as though he'd grown up in the neighborhood instead of being a guy she'd met twice. "Geoff, I'm so glad you could make it."

She took his coat, relieved him of the wine he'd brought and gestured to the wrapped gift in his hand. "You didn't have to bring all this. But there's a gift table in the dining room. Everyone's in the living room, go on down there and Jack will get you a drink."

"Thanks."

He dropped off the gift as instructed and followed the sounds of a party. Got to the doorway and stopped almost as though a blow had stunned him.

Iris in Bloom

Iris sat in a chintz armchair, nothing sexy about that, but she absolutely shimmered. Her face was alight with laughter as she talked to the way too good-looking guy at her side. Her eyes sparkled, her teeth gleamed as she laughed, her hair tangled with the candlelight, gleaming gold and red. She wore a dress the color of the summer sky right when the light falls and it's a deep, dusky blue. Brought out the color of the stone at her neck and her blue eyes.

He'd never seen her legs before and he thought that a woman with legs like that shouldn't be allowed to cover them up with jeans and pants. It was a crime. They were meant to be displayed exactly as they were now, with a dress and those sexy heels.

"Geoff, glad you could make it," Jack Chance boomed across the room.

He still couldn't take his eyes off Iris. When she heard her father's words she glanced quickly up and their gazes connected. He felt the second punch to the gut and he knew right then that whatever happened, he did not want to be friends with this woman. In spite of the complications in his life. He wanted more. A lot more.

It took Jack's clap on the shoulder to pull him out of his trance. "Thanks for inviting me," he said, and they shook hands.

"What can I get you? It's a full bar and we've got beer and wine and—"

"A beer would be great. Thanks."

While his host went to fetch his drink, he walked over to Iris. "Happy Birthday," he said. He leaned forward and kissed her cheek. Once more her scent assailed him, the sugar and spice of her and some exotically darker note beneath.

"Thank you."

Then she turned to the GQ model sitting beside her who was looking Geoff up and down with more than casual interest. "Evan Chance, this is Geoff McLeod. Geoff is the new high school English teacher. And Evan is my big brother."

Feeling much more disposed to like the guy now he knew he was her brother, Geoff held out his hand.

"How do you like Hidden Falls?" Evan asked him.

"I like it. I'm settling in. Jefferson High's a good school. I haven't seen you around."

"No. I live in Miller's Pond, a couple of hundred miles from here. It's a good place too."

"What made you move from a small town in Oregon to an even smaller town in Oregon?" The guy did not look small town.

A look of mixed emotions, some pride, some embarrassment, some amusement crossed his features. "A woman."

"The right woman," Iris added.

Geoff followed the brother and sister glances and the whole story was written there. "The right woman," he agreed.

Then Evan rose. "I'm going to see if I can help Mom in the kitchen. Maybe we can catch up later." And he vacated the chair next to Iris.

"Nice guy," Geoff said sitting beside her, appreciating the tactfulness of her brother.

"He's the best."

"You look beautiful tonight. You sparkle."

She laughed. "It's hard not to sparkle when people you love put on a nice party for you and bring presents and make food." She raised the glass in her hand, as sparkly as she was. "And open champagne."

Jack Chance brought him his beer and stopped to chat for a moment. "I'm sorry we didn't get more of the kids home." He sighed. "Seems like every birthday we have fewer of the brood home. You're all growing up, moving away, having busy lives."

"I got emails and phone calls from every one of them," Iris said, obviously trying to cheer her dad up. "Prescott sent me an architectural drawing of my house. He must have taken it from a photo when he was last here. It's gorgeous."

"He's a good boy. But he should come home more often."

"Wait a second," Geoff said. "Prescott Chance is your brother?"

"One of the many."

"Prescott Chance the architect?"

"You've heard of him?" She sounded amused.

"Who hasn't? The guy's legendary."

"Well, to me he's a brother. Mostly, I remember him saying, 'I don't have to do what you say. You're not the boss of me.'" She imitated a surly kid pretty well.

"From what I read, no one's the boss of him." Not that he knew much about architecture but it was kind of like having royalty or a pop star or something in the family. He kind of liked that nobody made a big deal of it.

"I'm sorry you couldn't meet him," Jack said.

Daphne Chance breezed in to announce that dinner was all set up on the dining table and for everyone to help themselves and sit wherever they could find a spot.

"Iris," she said, "You go first."

"Oh, no, really."

"You have to, Dear. You're the birthday girl."

With a helpless shrug, she left him and headed for the buffet table. Since his own mother would have his hide if he took food ahead of anyone female or older than him, Geoff waited. He didn't mind. It was nice to have an opportunity to see her home, her family and friends.

Daphne appeared and took the chair Iris had vacated. "She's a published author, you know," she said as though she were aware that he was watching her daughter.

He dragged his attention from the way that dress fit Iris, the way it emphasized some very nice curves.

"Iris? An author?" She'd never mentioned it. Interesting.

"Yes. She was published in a couple of prestigious magazines."

"Really? I didn't know that."

"That's Iris for you. She always hides her light under a bushel." She shook her head fondly. "So you haven't read any of her stuff?"

"No. But I'd like to."

She grinned at him as though they were conspirators. "Come with me." She led him out of the main living area and into a library/den/study/sewing room bursting with books and magazines and board games. Two desks and two computers sat on a long desk that looked like a very long plank of wood with some home made legs supporting it. He could imagine the Chance brood doing homework in this room.

Daphne went to one of the overcrowded bookshelves and she pulled out a copy of Atlantic Monthly, bound in clear plastic to protect it.

"Iris was published in the Atlantic Monthly?"

She nodded. "She's very good."

He flipped to the page. Barely got to start reading "Gingerbread Chess," by Iris Chance, when Daphne was handing him a photocopied version, clipped with a staple that had gone in crooked.

"Take it with you."

"Thanks." He'd love to sit quietly and read Iris's story to the end, but he was at a party, so he folded the pages neatly and slipped them into his pocket.

He'd only read a couple of paragraphs and already he was fascinated, about what it revealed about the author as much as the quality of the prose.

Chapter Nine

Even though it was Iris's birthday, as Geoff watched the family dynamic he noticed that when she was with her siblings and her friends, she did more listening than talking.

And when he was near oftentimes she was either listening to complaints or fears or problems or offering advice.

He was helping himself to seconds when he caught sight of a pencil sketch that showed a much younger Jack Chance, but the subject clearly was Jack Chance. He had long hair in the sketch and seemed so peaceful he could be sleeping. The piece was signed, Daphne Naigle. It was dated 1976.

"She drew that the day we met," Jack Chance said, pausing beside Geoff. "I insisted on having it framed and hanging it here where I can see it every day. Reminds me of what a lucky man I am."

"How long was it before you knew…" He didn't know how to end the sentence without sounding like a sentimental fool.

"Before I knew she was the one? The love of my life?" Iris's dad clearly had no issues about sounding like a romantic fool. "Let's see. I climbed on a Greyhound bus north of San Francisco. Saw Daphne right away. By the time we got to Portland, probably, I knew.

"You fell in love within hours?"

The older man grinned. "Minutes if you want to know the truth." He sent Geoff a look that suggested he saw more than Geoff wanted him to. Like he was sizing him up as a possible son-in-law. "That's how it happens sometimes. If you're lucky." And he slapped Geoff on the back and heeded his wife's call to help him in the kitchen.

After Geoff had eaten far too much and then been served a slab of strawberry shortcake the size of a road paver, Daphne announced that it was time for presents.

"No, Mom," Iris protested. "Nobody wants to watch me open gifts."

"Yeah. We do." Cooper said in his boisterous way. Cooper was the youngest boy, he'd told Geoff when he introduced himself and though he was in grad school he didn't seem like he took life too seriously. "And if I don't get major kudos, my present's going back to the store."

So Geoff found himself part of a circle watching Iris open gifts.

There were the obvious no-imagination presents of scarves and bath products. A Kiss the Cook apron, some chocolates, but those were mostly from old friends and she acted delighted with everything. Her mother handed her a large box and said, "It's for the café but if you don't like it you know I won't mind."

Iris opened the box and cried out with unfeigned delight. She lifted out an enormous ceramic sunflower with a clock mechanism. "I love it. It will look perfect on that big blank wall." Then she and Daphne posed for a photo with the clock.

From her sister Rose, the doctor, she got a card. When she opened it and read the contents she blushed and said, "No, it's too much."

Her sister shook her head. "The first one's on me."

"Wow. Thanks."

He wondered what that was about. The first what? Figured he'd probably never know. It was likely some obscure cosmetic procedure he didn't need to hear about.

When she got to his present, she glanced up in distress and said, "Oh, Geoff, you didn't need to get me anything. Not when my mother roped you into coming."

"Happy to be here. I wanted to."

He found that he was excited to see her open the gift, as excited as he'd been when he spotted it. Okay, he hadn't casually spotted it, he'd tracked it down online and driven all the way to Portland to pick it up.

He wasn't the type to wrap things obscurely to hide what they were so it was quite obvious the wrapping covered a book.

When she ripped off the wrapping she said, "Oh." She held it up. "Progress of Love, Alice Munro." She opened it almost as though she were going to start reading right there and then and she squealed. "It's a signed first edition!"

The book hadn't been particularly expensive but he'd wanted the gift to be special. He was pretty sure he'd succeeded in the birthday present department.

"Geoff." Her face lit up as he'd hoped it would. "I can't believe you found this. I love it." And she ran across the room to hug him. "Photo," she cried. "I need a photo."

When he would have risen, she perched on his lap holding the book toward her brother who snapped pictures. He slipped an arm around her waist and posed.

Before she left his lap, she turned her head. Their faces were inches apart. "Thank you," she said softly and kissed him briefly on the lips.

When the gifts were done people started to drift away, gathering coats and leaving. He judged it was time for him to take his leave.

"Thanks for a great evening, Daphne and Jack," he said to his hosts. He turned to Iris, felt that sizzle once more. "Happy Birthday again."

"Thanks. I'll see you out."

And so she walked him to the door. They found his coat and he hesitated, wanting to kiss her so badly it hurt but, knowing she'd made it clear she wanted to be friends, and besides her family was inside. He settled for a hug. A long hug that had a lot of sensations to it that did not scream friend.

As he trudged off toward his car, he heard her say, "Mom, Evan's parked behind my car. Tell him to move it."

He heard her mother respond, "He and Caitlyn have gone to bed already." There was a short pause. "I don't want to disturb them."

"No. They're probably having sex." She made an irritated sound. "How did he not know that was my car? How am I supposed to get home?"

Geoff felt the evening was about to take a decided uptick when he turned back to the house. "I can give you a ride home. It's on my way."

She stood in the doorway, backlit, so all he saw was her silhouette. Even the shadowy curves thrilled him. "Are you sure?"

"I'm sure. Want me to wait?"

"No. I'm ready to leave."

He headed back to the house. "I can do Sherpa duty then. Help haul the loot."

So, he went back inside and helped her carry her presents to his car.

"I'm really sorry about this," she said.

"It's fine. I'm glad to have you to myself for a while."

He had a way of saying things like that in such a normal tone that it was hard to be completely certain that he was hitting on her, especially as they'd agreed to be friends.

"I hope that wasn't too weird, getting steamrolled by my mother into coming to my birthday party."

"I'm glad she asked me. I like your family, and your friends seem nice."

"They are."

"I'm happy to be one of them." He said it with a sideways glance that she could take to be irony if she wanted to. Or she could assume he was being straight.

"I'm glad to have you as a friend too." She sounded forced even to her own ears like she was trying too hard to believe the words.

Which would be the truth.

Since he'd never been to her house she gave him directions as they drove. When he pulled up in front of her place, she felt a tiny fritz of awkwardness. Invite him up for coffee? That would seem like she wanted sex. Lean over and kiss him on the cheek? What if he thought she was going for his mouth and lunged at her? Get out and slam the door behind her?

He opened his car door and got out while she was still trying to figure out how to say goodbye. He flipped the trunk and she recalled the gifts. Right.

Of course he was coming in. He was her gift Sherpa.

Between them they got everything in one load. She led the way up the two steps to her front porch and managed to unlock the door and get it open.

She flipped on a light switch with her elbow and walked through to her living area to deposit her gifts on the table in there. Geoff followed behind her and similarly bestowed packages and boxes.

When she straightened he was very close to her.

The door was still wide open and she could hear a neighbor's dog barking. Probably telling the neighborhood that she was home.

"Do you want some coffee—that always seems like such a strange thing to offer a person this time of night. A caffeinated beverage. I have herbal tea." She was babbling she realized.

"I would love some herbal tea."

She was about to list off all the kinds she kept in the house, as though she were in the café, when she caught herself. "What kind do you like? I probably have it."

She shut the front door as she walked toward the kitchen and he followed her. "Whatever kind you're having is fine."

"Chamomile?" Calming.

"Sure."

Her kitchen was her favorite room and probably the reason she'd bought the house. Not large, it boasted top of the line appliances and extra wide granite countertops perfect for a woman who loved to cook. The extra width meant she could leave the appliances she used most often – and there were a lot of them – out for ease of access.

The kitchen flowed through into a den with a fireplace. Geoff wandered in there now to check out the jammed floor to ceiling bookcases that covered every inch of wall.

She left him to it and got on with making the tea. When she had two cups of chamomile brewed to perfection she put honey and napkins on a tray and brought the whole thing over. By this time Geoff was settled comfortably on the couch, his feet up on the table reading. Exactly the way she read. He'd even flipped on the reading light. When she glanced to see which of her books he'd chosen, she noticed he had a stack of photocopied pages in his hand.

Photocopied pages look pretty much the same but the coincidence of him having been in her parents' house and the appearance of this size stack of pages had her groaning. "Tell me she didn't."

"If you mean, did your mother share one of your published short stories with me then yes, she did."

"Does every mother wake up in the morning wondering how they can embarrass their kids or is it only mine?"

The twinkle was back in his eye. "Probably only yours." He thumbed the stack against his knee. "I haven't read very far but this is really good stuff. I can't believe you didn't tell me you're an author."

"Mostly I make coffee and baked goods these days, but thanks."

"Are you still writing?"

"Yes." Sort of.

He shifted so he could see her more clearly. "Good. What are you working on?"

She blinked. "Don't you know that most writers hate that question?"

"I'm sorry. I teach creative writing too. I get so used to grilling my students. I forgot."

"It's okay." She settled on the couch beside him. "I'm working on a linked series of short stories set around the café. They'd be fictional obviously but every day there are dramas in that café. I'm having fun with it but obviously writing a full length novel is more work than a short story." She shrugged realizing it had been a while since she had sat down and really worked seriously on her novel. It seemed too easy to let life get in the way. "Now that I'm thirty-three I should get more serious about my writing schedule."

"You definitely should."

"You doing the teacher thing again? Cause I gotta tell you that's annoying."

"You know what you should do?"

"Do not tell me to read Stephen King's book on writing and then write ten pages every day. That only works if you're Stephen King."

"Okay. Point taken. Actually, I was going to ask you to come and talk to my creative writing class."

He sipped his tea. She'd given him the most manly of Daphne's pottery mugs but this one kind of listed to the side like the leaning tower of Pisa.

"You want me to talk to your creative writing class?"

"Yes."

"But I run a bakery."

"You're a published author. You could encourage budding authors."

"Are there any budding authors at Jefferson High? Must have changed since I went there."

"You don't know when a seed will bear fruit."

"You want me to come and seed young minds."

"I do."

She really did need to get back to something she used to love. Maybe this would be the kick in the pants she needed. "Okay," she said. "I will."

"Fantastic. Class is an hour. Prepare something so you can teach them an element of storytelling, then maybe have a writing exercise and a few questions. It would be amazing to have a real author at the school."

"It's been a while since I thought of myself that way." Maybe she needed to make time.

"You're too good to let it go."

"What have you read, a page?"

"Couple of pages. You caught me at the first line."

"Thanks." Okay, she was good. She knew she was good. But after the heady success of having two short stories published she then started getting rejections. Markets closed. Magazines stopped publishing. Somewhere along the way, she'd stopped writing every day.

He interrupted her thoughts to say, "Was it a good birthday?"

"It was."

They both sipped tea which caused a moment of silence.

"How's this friends thing working for you?" he asked when he'd returned the leaning mug to the table.

"Fine."

"Because I have to tell you it's not working for me at all."

She experienced a sudden pang of distress. Why didn't he want to be her friend? Was it her embarrassing mother? Her family? Maybe he thought she'd taken too much of the spotlight tonight. "It's not?"

"No."

"You don't want to be my friend?"

He seemed to mull over the question. "Friends isn't top of mind where you're concerned."

"Oh." She saw the man-woman thing in his eyes, the way he was gazing at her mouth and realized that whatever she claimed, it wasn't friendship she felt when he was around, either. "What, um, what would be top of mind?"

"This." He reached forward, slowly enough that she could pull away, but strangely she didn't. She watched his mouth until he was so close her eyes drifted shut. When he pulled her into his arms she let herself go, melting into him. His lips took hers with command, passion, need. She felt an answering need in her body. Wrapping her arms around him she pulled him yet closer.

He felt good. Solid. He smelled like clean, healthy male with a darker note beneath that smelled like desire.

He made her feel things she hadn't felt in a long while, and on this birthday when she'd felt bad about her first gray hair and compromised fallopian tubes he reminded her that she was still young and vital and the urges surging through her were strong and good.

When he deepened the kiss, she heard a soft sigh and realized it came from her. He tasted of the evening, of beer and a hint of strawberry overlaid with chamomile.

Not so calming tonight, that chamomile.

They kissed for a while and she could feel herself growing hot and restless. She hadn't had sex since Rob and that had been more than six months ago. Her body reminded her that it had needs that weren't being met.

Needs. And that a man currently on her couch kissing the sense out of her would definitely be up for the job. But all the reasons why she'd decided it was a bad idea got in the way.

"We," she gasped, "Should--"

"Oh, yes, we definitely should."

"Stop," she said.

It took a second for the message to reach his brain. He pulled away, looking as horny as she felt. "I must have heard wrong, I think you said, we should take this to the bedroom, but I heard stop."

She made a sound of frustration and want and why couldn't this amazing man be free?

"I did say stop."

He pulled back, ran a hand through his hair. "Okay. You want to tell me why?"

"It's all the same reasons as before. You're not free. And I don't want to be some transition woman or, even worse, the vehicle you use to get even with your wife."

He looked as frustrated as she felt as he rose to his feet, and then picked up her story from where he'd left it on the coffee table.

"I'm trying to be understanding about this but there's nothing I can do about the fact that I'm technically married. Believe me, I'm getting divorced as fast as I can."

"What if she changes her mind?" she said, rising too. "What if she and your friend realize they've made a terrible mistake and she asks you to come back?" There it was. Her darkest fear around him.

As he was leaving he turned back and said, "I don't know a lot about the future but one thing I can promise you. I am never going back to my wife."

Chapter Ten

The smell was the same, Iris thought, as she pushed through the double doors into Jefferson High. She'd been back a couple of times for various events and once when she took an accounting course at night school. But she hadn't really spent any amount of time here since she'd been a student. It smelled like a combination of teenaged sweat, anxiety, hormones and whatever they cleaned the floors with.

Since class was in session it was strangely quiet. She could hear her boots echo on the linoleum as she headed for the office as Geoff had instructed her.

After the awkward way he'd left, the night of her birthday party, she'd wondered if he'd come in for his usual coffee and what she'd do if he did.

And what she'd do if he didn't.

He'd come in Monday morning like always and if he wasn't exactly the same with her, he was almost the same. On Tuesday, he'd said, "How's next Monday for you?"

"Pardon?"

"To speak to my class? You can come Monday in the morning or Wednesday last block." He took his first sip of coffee as though it were the only thing between him and a coma.

So, here she was, hoping her two published short stories gave her some authority to share what little knowledge she had.

"I'm speaking to Mr. McLeod's creative writing class," she told the woman behind the counter who she didn't recognize. She gave her name and received a visitor's badge.

"Have a seat. I'll page him."

"Thanks." She settled in one of a line of plastic chairs. At the end of the line a kid with a lot of hair and a jittery knee looked to be waiting to see the principal. She felt momentarily insecure. Were the jeans too much? Did she look like she was trying to fit in with kids half her age? Show them she was cool?

But she always wore jeans. It was as stupid to dress up for them as it was to dress down.

She had notes in her bag and resisted the urge to read them over one more time. She'd be fine.

It was Geoff himself who came to collect her from the office. She'd thought he might send a student. He smiled when he saw her, that warm, intimate expression she felt was only for her. "Hi."

"Hi."

"Thanks for coming. The kids are wildly excited."

"Wildly excited?"

"Sure. It's one hour they don't have to listen to me."

She rose and he held the door for her to go ahead of him.

She walked with him into the classroom and found about thirty kids assembled. They slouched at desks, were skewed around so they could talk to their neighbors, generally seeming less than thrilled to be here.

"Okay, class. Listen up," Geoff said and the kids immediately straightened, stopped chatting and faced forward. Sign of a good teacher, she thought. He had their respect.

"I want to introduce you to Iris Chance who is with us today because she's a published author. You've all read her short story, "Gingerbread Chess," so if you have questions I'm sure she'll answer them."

They'd read her story? She supposed it made perfect sense but she wished he'd warned her.

"Raise your hands if you have questions. Ms. Chance, the floor is yours." And he walked to the back of the room and sat down in one of the student desks.

"Thank you for having me," she said. Already a hand was in the air. She'd planned to talk about short stories and about character development but it seemed they were already at the Q and A portion. "Yes?"

The girl asking the question was a pretty brunette. "Did you always know you wanted to be a writer?"

"What's your name?"

"Rosalind."

"Thanks, Rosalind, that's a good question. No. I don't think I did. I always liked books and stories. I was an avid reader as I'm sure you all are. I got an idea when I was in college. I wrote it and sent it in to a few magazines. I was really lucky to get published. I wrote some more short stories. Some were accepted for publication and some weren't."

She glanced around the room. She felt some interest and a lot of apathy. One kid in the back wore a ball cap over black curly hair. He'd settled back in his seat, slouching, like he was settling in for a nap.

"You write about a woman searching for her adoptive parents. Is it your story?"

She licked her lips. She had not anticipated that Geoff would share her story or that she would be grilled on its content. But she was here. She wasn't going to lie. "Yes. Yes the story was based on my own experience."

"Did that really happen? Did you really find out that your adopted mother was a drug addict and that your dad was in jail?" The same girl asked the questions. She didn't mean to be insensitive, Iris reminded herself. She was young.

Iris took a moment to formulate her answer. "When we write fiction we make things up. That's why it's fiction and not non-fiction. However, stories come from somewhere and in some way they are always about us. Or they offer some metaphor for what's going on with us. So, while the story did come from my own attempt to find my birth parents, the people in the story and the events were made up."

"What about the emotions?" a kid in back asked without raising his hand.

"What's your name?"

"Dylan." He dragged out each syllable turning two into four.

"Well, Dylan, the emotions were pretty real, I'd say. I probably used writing that story as a kind of therapy."

"It's really good," a sunny looking blonde at the front of the class said. And before Iris could ask her name she said, "I'm Bethany."

"Thanks, Bethany."

"How does it feel to find out you're adopted?"

Geoff must have sensed her discomfort. He said, "I'm not sure that's relevant, Bethany. Ms. Chance is here to talk about writing not her personal life."

"It's okay," she said. And realized it was. "I have an amazing family. Jack and Daphne Chance took kids in and never, ever differentiated between the ones they conceived and the ones they picked up along the way. They left it to us if we wanted to know."

She thought back. "I wanted to know. I was having a bad time with my mother." She grinned realizing she'd been the age of the kids in this class. "You know what that's like, right? I was positive the woman making me crazy wasn't my mother. At first, when I found out she wasn't, I was happy. And then I went looking for my birth family."

She glanced around. "Let's say I realized I was very lucky to end up where I did. But I think when you find out the people who gave birth to you didn't want you, it's always going to be hard."

A hand went up. Thank God. "Yes?"

"I'm Stefan. I'm adopted too."

"Are you okay with it?"

"I know who my real mom is and yeah, I'm okay with it."

"Good. That's good." She glanced at the clock on the wall. Noticed a collection of literary action figures and wanted to laugh. "I was going to talk about inventing character but since you've read my story you've seen how you can take something that happens in your life and write about it. You now know that it's based on something real, but as an author you still create character. You need conflict, good descriptions."

"What's the most important thing if you want to be a writer?"

"You have to write. Writers write." She felt like a fraud saying those words realizing she'd let that slide in her life. "Someone once asked Sir Edmund Hilary how you learn to climb a mountain. You know what he said?"

Silence and a couple of uh-uhs.

"You know who Sir Edmund Hilary is, right?" she asked, feeling old. She was almost certain the kid in the back with the ball cap rolled his eyes.

"First white man to climb Everest," the boy named Dylan said.

"Right. He said you learn to climb a mountain by climbing mountains. Writing's the same. You learn to write by writing. And reading, of course. A lot of people write a journal or you can write fiction."

She glanced at the clock and realized the hour was speeding past. "Let's try an exercise. Take a moment in your life. Something that happened that was significant and write about it. Take ten minutes and try to use every sense. Sight, smell, hearing, taste, touch." She heard the rustle as books were opened, pens unearthed.

Because she also had ten minutes to kill, she settled herself into Geoff's desk and pulled out her own pen and paper. She saw, to her secret delight, that he was doing the exercise too.

She wrote about her momentary embarrassment at being grilled by the students on the personal aspects of the story she'd written.

She'd forgotten that feeling of being pulled into the world of words. She struggled for the first minute and then felt the flow. If she hadn't set the timer on her phone she'd have flown past the time limit.

"Okay," she said, when her phone beeped, putting down her pen. "How was that?"

A few mutters of fine and okay met her ears.

"Good. Anyone want to share?"

She felt the blank wall hit her. Then Rosalind, the girl who loved the sound of her own voice put up her hand. She read a short piece about getting chewing gum stuck in her hair. That girl was no Thurber but it was mildly amusing.

"I really liked the way you involved all five senses around the piece of gum," she said. "You had the taste, the smell, the feel of it in your mouth and in your hair, the touch as you tried to pull it out, even the sound of the scissors cutting the gum out of your hair. And of course, the appearance. Nicely done."

"Thanks." Rosalind tossed the now gum-free hair over her shoulder, well satisfied with herself.

"Anyone else?"

One boy read a paragraph about a girl he dreamed of. One girl got choked up reading about a cat that died.

Ball-cap boy now definitely had his eyes closed. Maybe she wasn't a real teacher but she wasn't having anybody sleeping while she was trying to share her knowledge.

"You, boy in the back with the black curly hair."

It took a minute before he opened his eyes. He lifted his head. "Yeah?"

"I would like you to read what you wrote."

He shrank a little in his seat. "I don't want to."

"Reading might wake you up."

He muttered something. Then, in a monotone voice he began:

"Every morning he lifts the thousand pound weight of his head off the pillow. His chest is bare because the tattoo is so fresh it hurts to touch. It stings when his tears run over it in the night. Salt into the wound. He had them carve her name into his chest. It sounded like a dentist's drill, smelled like a butcher's. Drops of blood bubbled around each letter like his heart was crying."

She and Geoff exchanged glances of astonishment. There was dead silence for a moment, as though no one had

91

known that the quiet kid in back had such poetry in him. "That was amazing." She walked a step forward. "What is your name?"

"Milo."

"Okay. Apart from the senses, name one technique Milo used brilliantly." Hell, there were about ten so it shouldn't be hard to find one.

"It made me feel really sad," one girl offered.

"Right. He evoked emotion."

Silence.

"How about metaphor? He uses the tattoo as a metaphor for the way experience carves itself into our memories."

She was sorry when class ended. The bell cut them off mid question and Geoff rapidly thanked her and the class clapped even as they were packing up and banging and slopping their way out of the room.

"Milo," she called out before he disappeared.

"Yeah?" He glanced at the floor.

"I—you are really talented."

He shrugged and looked uncomfortable. Following a spurt of inspiration, she said, "Come and talk to me sometime. I run the Sunflower Tea and Coffee Company. I would love to read more of what you've written."

"Sure, yeah, maybe." He looked mortified at the idea. Another boy nudged him and muttered something and a few people around laughed. She didn't need to hear the words to figure it was something rude.

And he shuffled out, all that creativity hidden in a slumping gait and black clothes.

Then the room was empty but for her and Geoff.

"Phew," she said.

"That went really well," he said, rising from the student desk and coming forward. "They connected with you."

"I had fun. Did you know Milo had so much—"

"I had no idea. He always seems like he's miles away, thinking of somewhere he'd rather be."

"Who knew that talent was hiding right here."

Geoff looked at her curiously. His eyes looked ridiculously blue today since he was wearing a blue shirt. "What are you going to do with him at the coffee shop? If he comes."

"I don't know. It was a spur of the moment offer. If he's got more writing and he's serious, I could mentor him."

"He's a lucky kid."

"Plus, what if he didn't dream up that scenario, what if he's really struggling with a breakup or depression or something."

Geoff's blue, blue eyes narrowed slightly as he scanned her face. "Is he coming to you for mentoring or therapy?"

What was that supposed to mean? "I'd like to help him if I can."

That night while she was scanning more potential sperm donors, her email chimed.

It was from Geoff. He said:

Thanks again for today. The kids really liked you.

So did I.

You know what I wrote about in my ten minutes?

You.

Chapter Eleven

The weather forecast for the weekend was sunny and unseasonably warm for early April.

It was a Friday afternoon and, on impulse, she called Geoff. They were friends, after all. After she'd made it clear that's all she wanted, he hadn't made any attempts to get close to her again.

In fact, apart from seeing him every day when he came in for his morning coffee, and that one day talking to his creative writing class, she hadn't really seen him at all.

Dosana had the day off as she had an exam and there was no one in Sunflower so on impulse, she called Geoff.

She hated to think of him alone on a sunny weekend.

He picked up right away. "Geoff McLeod."

"Hi Geoff, it's Iris," though of course he knew it was her.

"What's up?"

She could hear noise, laughter, music. Voices. "Did I catch you at a bad time?"

"No. Some of the teachers go out after work on a Friday afternoon is all."

She heard a female voice with a distinct Texas drawl in the background. Seemed like he wasn't so lonely after all. But she'd called him for a reason. If they were friends, his dating life was nothing to do with her.

"It's supposed to be nice Sunday. I was thinking of going on a hike and wondered if you want to come with."

"Don't people drink coffee on Sundays?"

"They do but without me serving it to them. It's my day off."

"Great. I'd love to. Text me the details." And he was gone.

Well, seemed like she needn't have worried about him sitting alone all weekend. She chided herself for being so bitchy. It was good that he was getting out and socializing with his colleagues. And if a certain physics teacher was along, it was nothing to do with Iris. Let Tara Barnes be his transition woman. Iris had made it clear she wasn't interested in the position.

Sunday dawned as sunny as the weather forecasters had predicted.

Since her dad was coming over to get started on the attic, she knew she had to get out. Jack Chance was funny. If you left him instructions, he wouldn't deviate from them and he was very good at the things he knew how to do. But if Iris was home, she'd hear the dreaded words, "Honey, can you come up here? I have an idea." And that would entail listening as he explained why it would be better if the bathroom was over by where she currently planned to put her desk and the closet should be turned into a sauna or something.

Therefore, she'd left him a list, a pot of fresh coffee, a sandwich in the fridge for his lunch and her cell phone number in case he really needed to get hold of her. Since Jack Chance didn't hold with cell phones she was confident he'd get on with the job at hand and not bother her unless strictly necessary.

She packed her daypack including an extra couple of wicked brownies since she always believed in rewarding herself for a workout. She'd told Geoff she'd pick him up on the way. She double checked she had everything, including her emergency medical kit and whistle and then headed out.

Not only was he ready when she arrived but he sported the well-worn gear of a seasoned hiker. Decent boots, technical fabric pants and layers on top. Two full water bottles sat like guns in a holster in the sides of his pack.

She nodded to herself. He'd do.

He strode up to the driver's side window. "You want me to drive?"

"Why?" Did he think she couldn't manage the mountainous roads in her own back yard?

"Because your car is so pretty and shiny and it's got your bakery logo detailed on it. Mine is an old Jeep that's already beat up. And it's got four wheel drive."

"Okay. Sold."

He pulled his old four wheel drive out of his spot and she parked in the newly vacated space then grabbed her pack and jumped into his passenger seat.

"Thanks for organizing this," he said and she watched his gaze scan her up and down, obviously checking that she was properly equipped the same way she had checked him out.

"You're welcome."

"I was surprised you asked me," he said.

"Hidden Falls is named after the very falls I'm taking you to. You can't live in Hidden Falls, and you certainly can't teach our children, and not have visited it."

He hit the main road and turned left. "Ah, I see. So this is a public service you're performing here."

"That's right. I'm doing my civic duty."

He sent her a sideways glance that looked brimful of deviltry. "What if I told you the local high school English teacher is really having trouble waking up every morning alone? Going to bed every night alone? What might your civic instincts suggest?"

She couldn't deny the quick rush of heat even though he was so obviously teasing.

"I'd say take a trip to the local animal shelter and get yourself a pet. Not a dog," she warned. "Not when you live in an apartment and work all day, but a cat maybe. Or a goldfish."

"A goldfish."

"Okay, a cat."

"I have a part time cat. It's not helping. I don't think you're being as sympathetic to my problem as you could be."

"You're going to take the next right turn," she said, happy that they'd got to the slightly tricky part where she needed to navigate to get him to the trail head.

A wooden post set at the back of a gravel parking area that would fit half a dozen vehicles informed them they were at the trailhead. One car sat in the parking area and a couple of mountain bikes were chained to the wooden post.

The ground was damp from recent rains but there was plenty of springtime in the air. She breathed in the sharp, fresh scents of evergreens and the mossy, earthy scent of the trail as they climbed.

As the trail grew steep they spoke less, but the silence was companionable, in spite of the way she'd been feeling around him ever since that steamy kiss.

When he hiked ahead of her, she watched his easy gait, the determined tread and the enticing broad spread of his shoulders.

When she took the lead, she felt his eyes on her back and felt him watching the sway of her hips as she moved.

It was early enough in the season, or maybe the updated forecast that had threatened a possible shower later in the afternoon had scared potential hikers away, but apart from passing a sole trail runner on his way back down, they had the trail to themselves.

The hidden falls weren't particularly well hidden. A signpost pointed the way and a well-worn path headed off the main trail. But the falls themselves were a sight worth seeing.

She felt a stab of local pride as Geoff stopped and looked up at the water cascading down, bouncing a few times into a series of pools before hitting the wide creek. Bright green moss adorned the sides of the canyon and the rock had slowly worn away to fantastic shapes. He looked around and said, "Wow. This is really incredible."

Even though clouds were gathering overhead, a beam of sun hit the falls sparking a wet rainbow.

"Come on, I'll take you to my favorite lunch spot," she said and led the way down a narrow rut that seemed to lead up a cliff. But abruptly, it took a turn and led them behind the falls.

"This is amazing," he said, peering through the curtain of water pounding in front of them. A fine spray of mist hit them as they stood close behind the falls, but when they backed off a few feet there were plenty of boulders to sit on and enjoy their sandwiches.

They munched happily for a few minutes.

"I hope my students didn't embarrass you the other day asking personal questions." He had to speak up so she could hear him over the falls.

"No. They were honest questions. I liked their openness."

"I don't want to pry, but did it happen the way you described in the story?"

She smiled wryly. "As I believe I mentioned in your class, I was writing fiction. We're supposed to make stuff up."

"And did you?" His face was ruddy from the fresh air and exercise, his eyes more gray in this light.

"Yes and no. The story is metaphoric." She let herself drift back to that awful time when she'd hoped for so much and learned such a bitter lesson. "My parents, Jack and Daphne I mean, always told us that when we were sixteen we could ask them anything and they'd tell us. Until then, no dice."

"I was seventeen when I started fighting with my mom. Usual stuff. I wanted more freedom, thought I should get the car more often, felt like I had too many chores to do. The usual. We'd been really at each other's throats one day and I decided I wanted to know who my real parents were. When I found out I was adopted, first of all, I felt triumphant. Like I was right all along – you know all those fairy tales where some poor hard-done-by maiden finds out she's really a princess. Anyhow, they'd made this deal with us and, even though I could see they didn't want to do it, they shared the information they had."

"Were you adopted through an agency?"

Nancy Warren

She snorted. "Not hardly. As you may have noticed, it's kind of alternative around here. Back then, I think there were a couple of communes. People who had babies and didn't want them could bring them to the Chances. That's what happened to me."

She took a long drink of her water. Strange how it still hurt to remember.

"I shouldn't have asked. You don't have to tell me. I'm as bad as Rosalind."

She shook her head. "It's okay. They had my mother's name and her last address. I contacted her. She lives in Seattle now. She seemed delighted to hear from me. We met at a restaurant." She could still smell the oily smell of fast food when she thought of that place. "I was too nervous to eat. I had tea. Mostly she talked about how much she and my father were in love and how much she regretted having to give me up."

She glanced up and saw the understanding in his eyes. "Everything I'd wanted to hear. She told me how beautiful I was and how proud she was of me."

He nodded.

"Then she shoved the contact details for my father at me. Said he'd be delighted to hear from me." She pushed half her sandwich back in its wrapping.

"Not so much?"

She shook her head. "Not so much. He's married. He was married back when he slept with my birth mother. Has another family. His 'real family' as he called them don't know anything about me. He answered some questions about his health background and made it clear he doesn't want to know I exist."

He reached out and grasped her hand. "In the story, he's in jail."

"That's how I saw him. Imprisoned in this lie he lives."

"The mother in the story's an alcoholic."

"I think my birth mother hoped she'd be able to get back with my birth father or maybe she simply thrived on the drama. I'm not really sure. Once she saw I wasn't going to get her what she wanted she lost interest."

"What awful people."

"And I share their DNA."

"You have an amazing family. That trumps genetic material in my view."

She chuckled. "You should hear Jack on the subject. He was a foster kid. He's all about taking responsibility for who you are and who you want to be."

"I like the person you turned out to be."

"Do you?"

"Yeah."

It had been growing increasingly cloudy as they sat eating their lunch but she'd been so caught up in her story that she hadn't noticed how bad it was getting until she heard the first crack of thunder. They both glanced up at the darkening sky.

"I think 'possible shower' in the forecast has been upgraded to 'storm,' she yelled. "We should head back before the rain hits."

He nodded and they swiftly packed up. She pulled out her rain jacket and was pleased to see he had one too. Like hers it was lightweight, meant to be kept stuffed in a pack for emergencies like this.

Their jackets were both meant for sudden squalls not for a pounding downpour that would challenge Gore-tex.

They reshouldered their packs and headed out, striding swiftly back to the main path that would lead them out of here.

The rain caught up with them before they reached the trail and it was the kind of rain the Pacific Northwest is famous for. The kind of rain that grows rain forests with evergreens hundreds of feet high.

The kind of rain that pounds the ground to slop and soaks through clothing to skin in minutes.

They marched out, but the rain drove down, soaking her hair and through her rain jacket to the layers beneath. Her feet stayed dry because she had excellent waterproof boots but they were the only part of her that did.

The storm wasn't right overhead and there wasn't much lightning and only a few booms of thunder. Mainly, it was a rainstorm.

By the time they'd half jogged, half slid their way to where the car was parked, they were both sodden.

"We need to dry off," he said as they threw their packs in the back of his Jeep and got inside. Water was running in rivulets down his face.

"If I go home my dad will get me involved in renovations I don't want to do."

"Then we'll go to my place. It's closer anyway."

The windows steamed almost immediately from their wet clothes. She felt water drip from her hair onto her soaking shoulders.

He cranked up the heater but even so they shivered. Rain bounced off the road surface, puddling in every dip. The windshield wipers couldn't keep up with the downpour.

He pulled up in front of his building and they sprinted for the door. Rain was bouncing off the asphalt, drumming into puddles.

They ran up the stairs and into his apartment.

"Ladies first," he said, pointing to the bathroom. "Clean towels under the sink."

She glanced down at her soaking clothing. A small lake was forming under her feet. "I have no dry clothes."

"I'll grab you some sweats. I've probably got something that will work."

"Thanks."

She unlaced and pulled off her boots, then peeled away the damp socks beneath. The pedicure she'd treated herself to on her birthday was still in great shape so her toes flashed like ten ripe cherries.

She hung her jacket on the hook by the door and stood dripping on the welcome mat until he returned with an armful of gray.

She grabbed the soft sweats and ran for the bathroom.

Her wet clothing clung as she undressed, hanging on with damp fingers. Even her underwear was soaked.

Naked and shivering, she ducked under a hot, hot shower and let the heat penetrate. She washed with his soap, shampooed with his shampoo, feeling absurdly intimate to be using the same bath products on her naked body that he used every day on his. As the water pounded down on her bare skin, she imagined for a second that he was in here with her.

Stop it! She kept the shower as short as she could knowing he was out there getting pneumonia waiting for her.

She toweled herself off swiftly with the fluffy blue towel she'd found under the sink, then took a moment to wring out her things. She'd put them in a grocery bag and take them home to wash.

She slipped into a gray T-shirt, gray sweat pants that, if she drew the drawstring as tight as it would go, didn't fall off her hips, and a sweatshirt that concealed the fact that she wasn't wearing a bra, which the T-shirt pretty much broadcast.

She finger combed her wet hair and emerged from the bathroom. "Your turn."

"That was amazingly fast," he said, looking impressed. "I was going to make coffee."

"I'll finish it," she said. "You shower."

He had a sack of coffee, the stuff he'd bought from her café, and he'd dragged out a French press. The kettle was close to boiling.

While he showered, she finished the coffee. He'd unearthed his sound system and she had to assume he'd put it on shuffle as Queen segued into Timberlake.

While the coffee was brewing, she wandered over to the living area. He'd managed to finish unpacking his boxes and the place looked a lot more settled.

There were a few photos on the wall, a guitar leaned in a corner.

The rain was not slowing. When she looked out the windows it was like being inside a cloud. Gray everywhere. If gray had a sound it would be the steady beat of rain on roof, on window, on the outdoor balcony. She felt the beat of it in the music, in the shower.

As she wandered by his desk, she saw his briefcase on the floor and assorted papers on the desktop. There were essays to be marked and a well-thumbed copy of King Lear sat out. She smiled. The poor kids. Lear again.

A lined piece of foolscap caught her attention. Hand written in ink and not in a student's hand, but his own. How do I tell her, it began.

With a start she realized this was his ten minute exercise from her class visit. She was already half way through before it occurred to her he hadn't given her permission to read his piece.

He'd told her in email, though, that he'd written about her.

How do I tell her that I think of her every morning? That I long for her the way I long for that first cup of coffee? I think of how she'll smile at me as I walk in and the metal sunflowers chime their greeting. I'll smell the coffee and the cinnamon and nutmeg from her baking. All those scents are part of her. When I brush my lips on her cheek I feel the softness of her skin and smell all the love that goes in to her work. How do I tell her that I want to taste her and touch her and feel every inch of her? How do I tell her?

She heard the bathroom door open and turned. As he stepped out, wearing a terry cloth bathrobe, she saw him start to say something and then realize what she was reading.

"Oh," he said. "I didn't mean for you to see—"

But she was already striding toward him, her gaze fixed on his and she didn't stop walking until her body was pressed against his.

"Tell me," she said and kissed him

Chapter Twelve

"I want you," he said simply when they pulled apart to breathe.

"Yes," she whispered.

"I want you in my bed."

"Yes," she said, kissing him again.

"I want you every morning when I see you in the coffee shop. I want to drag you in the back and make love to you in your kitchen."

"Oh, yes."

"When I had you in my classroom, I wanted to bend you over my desk and take you."

A rush of lust punched through her.

"Yes."

He took her hand and led her into his bedroom. The room was pretty much all bed. A gray linen duvet covered a brand new bed. On either side sat the tables she'd helped build. Amazingly, they were both still standing.

He kissed her long and slow, easing the sweatshirt over her head. Since the T-shirt clung to the gray fleece she let him peel the whole works off at once, thinking the rain had done half of the work of undressing her for him.

She pulled at the tie on his robe, as anxious to get him naked as he was to get her that way.

Mmm, he was nice. Broad shoulders, lean hips and a taut belly told her that he kept himself in shape.

He seemed as enthralled by her upper body as she was with his.

He flipped back the duvet and eased her down onto the bed, kissing her deeply. Once she was there, he reached for the waistband of the loaner sweats, tracing a fingertip along the line and untying the drawstring with slow, sexy care. Slowly, he eased them down her legs and pulled them off her.

"Oh, you are beautiful," he said, looking down at her stretched out naked before him.

His hair was still wet and it clung darkly to his head. The look in his eyes was everything she could want in a man perusing her naked body. He looked wowed, reverent and deeply lustful.

The combination had her skin heating up, her body feeling restless with need. It had been too long.

"Take off your robe," she commanded and with a swift grin he complied, dropping the garment to the floor with more speed than dignity so she was greeted to the sight of all of him, rock hard and eagerly jutting.

He climbed onto the bed with her and began to kiss her, his hands roving everywhere while their kisses deepened, grew hotter and wetter.

In fact, she was getting hotter and wetter in all the best places. Her hips began to dance in place, rubbing against him shamelessly until he groaned and pulled slightly back.

"I want to stretch this out all day," he panted, "but I don't think I can."

He reached for the drawer of the new night table she'd helped assemble and removed an unopened box of condoms looking a tad sheepish. "I bought these after you called."

"Were you so convinced I was a sure thing?"

107

He smiled down at her. "No. But in case you were I wanted to be prepared." And then he kissed her again and she lost the ability to tease.

His hands caressed her and wowed her and moved her ever closer to the brink until she could hear her own breath coming in heavy gasps.

"Ready?" he asked.

Words wouldn't form. She could only nod.

He ripped open the box, pulled out a square package and began to tear it open.

She made a move to stop him. More in instinct than conscious thought as she imagined all that lovely, baby-making sperm going to waste. Then, realizing what she was doing, dropped her hand.

"What?" he asked, breathing as heavily as she.

"Nothing."

"Don't you want to? We don't have to—"

"No! I do want to. I really, really want to."

"Okay." He looked at her doubtfully for a moment until passion overcame his obvious urge to quiz her on why she'd almost stopped him putting on a condom.

Of course an instant's reflection told her that – apart from the obvious health concerns – she had no business taking the man's seed without his permission. When she had all her senses back she'd take a moment to feel remorse but she knew that her instinctive reaction was exactly that. Some inner instinct to mate with a man who would give her healthy, strong and intelligent children.

In a second he was sheathed and once more began kissing her, this time, when she rubbed against that lovely hardness he didn't pull back, he pressed forward, entering her slowly, letting her enjoy the stretch and open to that lovely cock pushing all the way into her body.

When they began to move she felt a quiver run over his skin. First time since his wife, she realized dimly, giving him comfort as well as sex.

Then, because she didn't want him thinking about anyone but her, she held onto his jaw and looked right into his eyes, all the way into his very essence as their moves became faster, less coordinated. He didn't flinch. He stayed right with her, gazing into her eyes until she saw those gorgeous blue eyes lose focus and knew he was out of control. The knowledge fired her body so she was already convulsing around him when she heard him groan and pound into her a few times as he fell off the world with her.

She stayed beside him, resting her head on his sweat-damp chest, enjoying the pulses of her aftershocks as their breathing slowly returned to normal.

They didn't talk for a while, just lay there, listening to the rain and their own heartbeats and some soft music coming from the sound system that she thought might be Diana Krall.

After a while, he turned his head and grinned at her. "You get that out of the tantric sex book you were so taken with?"

"Get what?"

She couldn't remember one thing she'd read in her life and that included King Lear.

"The technique of looking your partner in the eye at climax. It's frighteningly intimate."

"Oh. No. I didn't even think of that. I wanted to make sure you knew who you were in bed with, I guess."

"Oh, darling. When a man's lucky enough to have you in his bed there's no room for anyone else."

She turned her head and bit his nipple lightly. "Good."

They lay there a little longer listening to the rain. He played with her hair.

"First time since your wife?" she asked.

There was a tiny pause. "Yes."

"You okay?"

He put a hand under her chin, tilted it so he could look right into her eyes. "I am so much more than okay."

A tiny smile pulled at her lips. "Okay, then."

Not letting her go, he said, "How about you?"

"I never slept with your wife."

"Very funny. How long since you were…intimate."

"About six months." Probably more like seven or eight if she got out a calendar and started counting.

"What happened there?"

She shrugged one naked shoulder. "It ended. Rob was a nice guy. No hard feelings on either side. Just didn't work out."

They stayed in for dinner. While the rain continued to pound down outside, she raided his fridge and freezer and made a respectable pasta dish from frozen shrimp and peas, some asparagus that was wilting slightly in the fridge, some cherry tomatoes and white wine, lemon, coffee cream and spices.

"This is fantastic," he said as he tucked in. Then he glanced up at her. "You're fantastic."

She shook her head.

"No. You are. I can't believe I found you."

She reached out and touched his hand. "Don't get too carried away. Remember, this is your first time out."

110

He stopped chewing to stare at her. "What's that supposed to mean?"

"Nothing. I'm only saying, you've been married for what? Six years? You're going to want to get out and date. It's natural."

She hated saying that. She felt like she was chewing on razor blades. But the sooner both of them were aware of the reality, the better.

"Why don't you let me be the judge of what's natural for me."

"Yeah. Sure."

"You know what I want right now?" he asked.

"No. What?"

"I want dessert." His eyes crinkled at the corners in a very sexy way.

"Well, we are out of dessert, Mr. McLeod."

"No lemon bars?"

She shook her head.

He rose from the table and started stalking her. "No wicked chocolate brownies?"

She shook her head, her skin already beginning to tingle.

"Then," he grabbed her and lifted her so fast she gasped, "I guess I'm going to eat you for dessert."

And he did.

She didn't mean to spend the night at Geoff's. It was the last thing she intended. The final time they'd made love she'd told him she needed to get home. He'd kissed her sleepily and agreed.

While their hearts settled to a more regular rhythm that seemed to thump in time to the rain on the roof, he said,

"When I came out of the shower and saw you at my desk, and you came right across the room and kissed me, was it—"

"It was the paragraph you wrote in class. You used every one of the five senses, by the way. Excellent work."

"I used every one of the five senses to describe how much I wanted you."

"You did."

He shifted, ran a hand over her breasts. "I wooed you with my words."

"You did."

"And I thought it was my hot bod."

She rolled so she was on top of him. "That too." And feeling sleepy and sexy and sated, she kissed him, her hair falling like a curtain around them.

The next sound she heard was his alarm dragging her out of the sweetest dream, one so nice she didn't want to leave it even though once her eyes were open she couldn't remember what had happened. She thought Geoff might have been in it. And she suspected from the tingling in her body that it had been an erotic dream.

He groaned. Opened one eye then the other flew open to join it. "I'm so sorry. I didn't think. You should be open by now. Come on. Let's get up. You've got to get going."

"No. I don't. Dosana's opening up. I'm going in later."

"But you're always there on the week days."

"I've got an appointment. Dosana knows."

"Oh. Okay." He didn't ask but obviously wondered what kind of appointment would take her away from her business.

Because he so carefully didn't ask she told him. "It's a medical test. No big deal. I'll be back for the lunch rush." Probably.

He grabbed a fistful of her hair and shook it gently. "You sure there's nothing I need to worry about?"

She shook her head. Smiled at him. "No. A routine thing. I'm healthy as a horse." Hopefully a mare in heat in fact.

She could hardly tell the man she'd gone through half a box of condoms with that she had an appointment with a fertility specialist.

Some things you didn't need to share with a brand new lover and she was reasonably certain that her plans to become pregnant through a sperm bank were right up there.

"Okay. You need a ride or anything?"

"No. But thanks for asking."

He kissed her swiftly. "I'm here."

She stared at him. Usually, that was her line.

Chapter Thirteen

"Congratulations," her doctor told Iris at her next visit. "We scanned your ovaries and you've got the eggs of a twenty year old."

"Well that's good."

"Sure is." The fertility doc tapped on a keyboard. "Next step is to see whether your fallopian tubes are open enough that you can conceive. It's a simple test. We shoot some dye into the tubes and check for blockages. If that's as positive as I suspect it will be then we're good to go."

"Why doesn't that sound as positive as I feel like it should?"

"Because I don't want to raise any false hopes. You're a good candidate for artificial insemination, no question. However, you have to understand that it doesn't always work."

"What are my odds?"

She'd asked Rose this same question but she wanted to see if both of the doctors she trusted were on the same page.

"Obviously, every body is different, but statistically, your chances of conceiving with AI are between ten and twenty percent."

Yep, her two trusted docs were on exactly the same page.

"So, statistically, if I try this five to ten times…?"

"I can't make any promises."

She nodded. And at several hundred bucks a pop, she was going to have to sell a lot of muffins.

She supposed she should be grateful that her chances were good that she could conceive instead of feeling that fate should have sent her a life partner by now.

"I want to get going on this." She had this strange sense of urgency, as though time was running out.

"Okay then. Here's the drill. You buy your sperm so it's ready when you are. You can schedule the procedure with my nurse for next week. If you're clear then on the first day of your next cycle, you're going to start taking your temperature."

By the time her doctor had finished, she felt like a science experiment. Pregnancy vitamins were first on the list. She was to start taking those right away.

Of course, if she walked into the local pharmacy and bought prenatal vitamins she might as well take out an ad in the Hidden Falls Record.

She'd have to drive to Eugene to get the vitamins and the fancy ovulation-detecting thermometer.

When she got to work later that day, Dosana appeared very happy to see her. "I was swamped this morning."

"Sorry."

"You think about more staff?"

"Yes. I'll do something. Put an ad on Craigslist, something. I promise."

"Okay."

She was icing the newest batch of cinnamon buns when the bell jingled. She put down the icing bag and went out front. It looked like one of the grim reaper's anorexic minions was out front. He was all in black, hunched into a black hoodie so all she saw was a pale oval of face. But she recognized that face and her own lit up when she recognized the promising creative writer from Geoff's class.

"Milo," she said. "You came."

"Yeah," he said to the floor.

"Come on in and have a seat. I'm really short staffed so I can't sit with you right away but let me give you a hot chocolate or a coffee or something and I'll be with you as soon as I can."

"Sure. Cool."

And he wafted to the back and sat at a table for two, pulled some books and a notebook out of his backpack and settled in.

Of all days, did he have to choose this one? Because she'd left Dosana on her own all morning, she'd felt guilty and let her employee off early as she had an exam to study for. Of course, the second Dosana left, every single citizen of Hidden Falls and way too many outsiders suddenly became overcome with caffeine withdrawal. As one, they converged on Sunflower.

She barely had time to think; all she could do was take orders, run the espresso machine. She'd never felt so close to losing it when she felt a presence behind her. Milo had one of the rubber tubs she used for dirty dishes and was hefting it, overflowing with dirty plates and cups into the back.

He didn't say a word, simply found a dishcloth and headed out front to wipe down tables.

On his next trip back, she shoved an apron at him. "Can you take this Panini to Eric? The guy with the red hair and the computer sitting in back?"

"Sure." He delivered the food and then returned. And from then on he ran food out, cleared, cleaned, swept. He couldn't run the cash register or the espresso machine and she wouldn't let him touch food, but it was so nice to have an extra pair of hands.

By four-thirty the rush ended as suddenly as it had begun.

"Phew," she said. "Thanks."

"No problem."

"You ever work in a coffee shop before?"

"No. I was a bus boy in the last place we lived in."

"You want a job?"

His vacant brown eyes lit for a moment. "You serious?"

"Yes, I'm serious. You helped without being asked and you have good instincts. I think you'd be an asset to Sunflower."

"I go to school."

She resisted the urge to roll her eyes. "I know. The job would be after school and weekends." Knowing that she did not want a lecture from his English teacher she hastily said, "And not every day, obviously. We'd work something out."

"Okay."

"Great. We'll get forms signed and so on, but for now, let's sit down." They settled at the table he'd already occupied. "Did you bring me any creative writing?"

He looked deeply uncomfortable. "Yeah."

"Good."

But still he made no move to get out his notebook or laptop or whatever he wrote on. Finally, he said, "I feel weird. I've never shown anyone my work before."

"But writing is meant to be shared," she said. "I can't tell you how much I learned in college from taking creative writing classes and then critiquing each other's work in class. Even simply hearing your work read aloud tells you something about whether the story's working or if the words flow."

"Do you even know how lucky you are, man?" a voice said from a few tables away.

Eric. He'd finished his Panini. Now, instead of working on the next great horror movie, he was eavesdropping.

He shook his head miserably. "You've got a published author sitting there wanting to read your work. That's like a gift. Take it."

Not only was Eric about as subtle as a solar eclipse, but his clear jealousy of Milo's chance worked on the budding writer. "I guess," Milo muttered and he reached into his pack and pulled out a dog eared notebook. Black, of course. Somehow she'd known he'd write in long hand. He pushed it toward her. Where other people might blush in embarrassment, he only grew paler, as though even his blood wanted to run and hide.

"Won't you read it to me?"

"Not where everyone can hear," he muttered.

She patted the notebook, completely understanding his position. Sure, they could meet somewhere else but she only had so much time and the coffee shop was where she usually was.

She leaned closer to Milo. "I'm going to try an experiment. If it doesn't work, we'll figure out something else. Trust me."

He looked slightly puzzled but shrugged which she assumed was permission to try her experiment.

"Eric," she said, "Would you like to read a scene from your screenplay?"

118

"Seriously?" If Milo went paler when he was embarrassed, Eric blushed enough for both of them. "Yeah. Sure. Okay."

He picked up his computer and his bag and lumbered over to their table, pulling up a third chair.

She wasn't sure her experiment was the greatest idea, but she liked his enthusiasm.

"Okay, so this is a horror movie. It's about zombie bats."

"Zombie bats. Okay."

"Yeah. The infection is coming from bats but no one knows that. They lock out the human zombies but you know, at night the bats come out."

"Oh, this is creepy," she said. "There's a reason I never watch horror movies."

"You'll never watch this one if I don't sell it," the screenwriter said.

"Read it," Milo said and she could see he was interested.

Eric started with his first scene and as he began to read aloud he stopped himself a few times. "No. That's the wrong word." Then, "Oh, man, no actor could spit all that out. I'll have to rewrite that line."

"See the value of reading your own work aloud? Or even better, having someone else read it."

"Would you?" Eric asked.

"What? Read your screenplay aloud?"

"Yeah. The two of you." He dug into his bag. "I've got extra scripts." He pushed two across the table. Assigned parts.

In moments she was saying words she'd never imagined would come out of her mouth.

"Chuck? Bolt the door. The zombies are coming. I can hear them. The army of death is on the march."

Chapter Fourteen

When Geoff walked into Sunflower at the end of the day he told himself he was only grabbing a latte and maybe one of those wicked brownies. He wasn't heading to Sunflower because he hadn't been able to stop thinking of Iris all day.

Caffeine and chocolate, that's what drew him.

Hot sex and a gorgeous woman? Nah.

He was rehearsing something cool and witty to say, not that anything was leaping to mind, as he walked in. Iris didn't even hear the bells. She and Milo and the red headed guy who seemed to live at one particular table in Sunflower were crowded around a table. Red had a laptop in front of him and Iris and Milo had screenplays. He knew they were screenplays from the way they were bound.

"Henry, what did ya do with the remote?" Iris read in a nasal, nagging tone. "Henry? Can't you say something when I'm talking to you? Henry?" Then she opened her mouth wide enough to scream and instinctively he ducked his head. But luckily she stuck to a silent scream.

"And scene." Eric said nodding. "Better that time, yeah. You guys were right." And he banged something into his laptop.

He didn't think he'd ever been overcome with lust before from watching a woman do a fake movie scream. This had to be a first.

"Okay," she said. "Milo, are you ready to read something now?"

"I think you should go first," Milo said.

She hadn't spotted him so he could watch her. Well, only the side of her face as she was facing Eric. But he felt the sudden tension in her body. Silence descended for a long moment. Then she said, "Okay. Okay, I will. Let me go get my laptop. I've got everything on there."

When she rose she saw him. And because he was looking he had the opportunity to watch her face when she first caught sight of him. He watched emotion jump into her eyes, surprise, lust, and like, and the awkwardness of here's this guy I had sex with last night, how do I act? She blushed a little, which only made him want to drag her into the back and do all the things to her he'd been fantasizing about since he'd kissed her goodbye this morning.

He wanted to reach out and touch her, to pull her into his arms so badly that he stuck his hands in his pockets to keep them out of trouble.

"Hi," she finally said.

"Hi."

It was one of those moments when neither moved or said anything and it seemed to stretch to forever. He felt himself reliving a storm of impressions from last night. Heat, and the sounds she made, and the look in her eyes when she climaxed and the way her chest blushed.

"I was going for my computer. Can I get you something?"

He knew a latte would take time and he didn't want to pull her away from her lit circle so he said, "Can you bag me a brownie?"

"Sure." She glanced around but the two male writers were deeply into it. He heard the words zombie brains and figured he could kiss her right in the middle of the coffee shop and the writers wouldn't notice. She must have caught the direction of his thoughts. She said, "Could you come in the back? I want you to look at, um, that thing I was telling you about."

"Absolutely."

He knew it was an honor to be invited to her inner sanctum. He glimpsed two ovens and racks of trays, stainless sinks and shelves of neatly labeled supplies.

He backed her up against one of the counters and kissed her breathless. "Was that the thing you wanted to talk to me about?"

She licked her wet lips. Nodded. Pulled him back for another long, deep kiss.

"Can you come over tonight?" he asked.

"I've thought about nothing else all day." He liked that she was honest about her desires. Flattered they were as strong as his.

"Me neither," he said.

He managed one more kiss before she collected her laptop and said, "I've got to get back out there."

As he left she put the CLOSED sign on the door behind him. Her sign said she closed at five o'clock but usually she wasn't as prompt.

He watched for a moment through the window, munching his brownie, as she sat and opened her computer. He watched her tap some keys and then take a deep breath and start reading.

She was discovering one of the truest rules of teaching, he thought. When you teach someone else, you always learn.

When Iris arrived home, she fully expected the house to be empty so she was shocked to hear the unmistakable sounds of construction upstairs. Banging and crashing keeping time with Led Zeppelin, which told her that Jack Chance was hard at work.

"Hi, Dad," she yelled up the stairs. "I'm home."

He turned off the music. "Honey, come on up here. I've been waiting. I want to talk to you."

Oh, no. Oh no oh no oh no! This only worked if she left him notes and he followed her instructions. She did not want to find tactful ways to tell him that his ideas were nutty. Her father was the Gaudi of home handymen.

This is my house, she reminded herself as she climbed to the upper level.

In spite of herself she cried out in pleasure. "Look how much you've done. Oh, that wide plank flooring looks so good in here."

"It does. I like the maple. It suits the house."

She glanced quickly around but nothing hideous hit her. Of course, he might be about to suggest they pull the roof off and replace it with glass to make that greenhouse he was so set on.

But what he said was, "I was looking at your plans. You've got this wall here so you'll have your office and then another room."

"I was thinking maybe a guest bedroom or a store room."

"I remember when you kids were small, we always liked to have a space where you could play that was near where we were working. Maybe you don't want a wall there. Maybe this could be a play area for the baby once it gets old enough, so you could keep an eye on it when you're working."

He sounded a little bashful and she knew that – even though his ideas were mostly terrible – it still hurt him to have them rejected. Also, she suspected that Mom had read him the Riot Act. He was to follow her instructions to the letter and not deviate.

She felt such a rush of relief and love when she realized that for once in his life, Jack Chance had come up with a brilliant idea. She nodded slowly, "Dad, that's so smart of you. Of course. There'd be room for a playpen and I can put a gate up by the stairs. This would be a fantastic play area."

He beamed with pride. "I can build you some shelves and cubbies to keep toys and games in."

"I like it. Let's do it."

After he left, she wandered the space. Her hand settled on her belly as she imagined herself doing paperwork up here while her child played nearby. Maybe this wasn't the way she'd planned her life, but she'd make it work. She knew she would.

Iris and Geoff fell into a routine. Her alarm went off much earlier than his, but he got up anyway and liked to share that first cup of coffee with her while she got herself ready. He laughed when he found out that she ate at home before heading to the café, but she always started her morning with oatmeal or a fruit smoothie at home. Otherwise she got so busy at work that she'd forget to eat.

Some mornings they woke at her place, some mornings at his.

She'd go off to the bakery, he'd head off to school. Some nights they'd head out of town for dinner, or he'd have marking to do and she'd cook dinner. Or she'd be working on her novel and Geoff would cook. Now that she and Eric and Milo had this unofficial critique group going, she was writing again. She hadn't known how much she missed it. Geoff wasn't the gourmet cook Iris was but he could manage to broil a steak or cook up a pot of pasta. And having a man cook for her was a big turn on she found.

She kept up with her friends and her usual activities, but nearly every night they ended up in bed together.

Meanwhile, she was sneaking her pregnancy vitamins and hiding in the bathroom to take her temperature, which she then had to mark on a sheet. She wouldn't be ready this month, but she was practicing hopefully the next cycle. Then, when her temp spiked it meant she was ovulating and she'd have to run down to be inseminated.

She was explaining all of this to her mother when Daphne said, "What does Geoff McLeod think of all this?"

Iris had one of those moments. It wasn't that she didn't know her mother was perfectly aware that her thirty-three year old daughter had a sex life, it was simply that she preferred not to discuss it.

"He doesn't think anything about it because he doesn't know."

"I'm sure it's occurred to you—"

"That Geoff McLeod could be my baby daddy?" She sighed. "Of course it has. And no. He's still married. The last thing he needs is a kid. He's trying to get his life back on track. We have fun together. That's it."

"Okay." Her mother said in a tone that pretty much meant: This is so far from okay you'd have to take a NASA shuttle to get there.

"Are you sick?" Geoff asked in alarm. He'd been on his way out the door and forgotten his phone, plugged into a wall socket in Iris's bedroom.

She was rifling through her closet when he walked in, a thermometer sticking out of her mouth.

She made a mumbling sound but didn't turn around. He waited, not wanting to be a man who abandoned a woman when she was sick. She stuck a finger in the air, as in wait one minute, and then dashed into the bathroom.

It seemed like she took a longer time than necessary to come out and when she did she looked a little flushed, like maybe she did have a fever.

He walked forward and put his hand on her brow, the way you do when someone has a fever, even though he could never tell unless they were absolutely burning up. And she wasn't.

"I'm fine," she said. Then, stepping out of his reach, added, "I felt a little off, that's all. Don't want to go into work and make half of Hidden Falls sick."

"No. You don't."

"I'm fine. No temperature."

"Good." He searched her face knowing something wasn't right but unable to figure out what it was. "So you're okay if I go off to the gym and leave you?"

"Yes. Go." She made shooing motions.

"Kay." He put his phone in his pocket. Turned back. "You know I only go to the gym so I can afford to eat all those treats at the bakery."

"I refuse to take responsibility for your lack of willpower," she stated, spoiling her nose-in-the-air pose with a laugh.

"Good. Because where you are concerned, I have no willpower." He showed her immediately how true that was by walking forward, grabbing her shoulders and pulling her to him for a deep, hungry kiss. He briefly wondered if he was giving himself flu and decided he didn't care. He'd risk a lot worse to show Iris how much she meant to him.

126

She melted against him, her body almost becoming part of his in a way he couldn't get enough of. Then she pulled slowly away.

"See you tonight?" he asked.

He watched her flip through her mental calendar. "I've got book club tonight. Which reminds me I have to pick up some wine."

He was amused. "Not a book?"

"Please, the book gets ten minutes. The rest of the time we drink wine and b—socialize."

He didn't press her, but silently hoped if there was bitching going on that it wouldn't be about him.

Chapter Fifteen

Geoff had an idea. Either one of his worst or his best he wasn't yet certain. He'd been watching the little literary circle developing in Iris's coffee shop. So far it contained four of his students. Including a girl who was crushing on Milo, and Milo was either oblivious or interested and being cool. Absolutely impossible to tell which.

Iris wasn't sitting around the table when he arrived.

"Hi Mr. McLeod."

"Hi kids. Don't mind me, carry on."

He headed to the counter where Iris's assistant Dosana was serving.

"Iris in back?"

"No." She barely spared him a glance. "She left."

For Iris to leave during a work day was strange, even more strange when she had the writing group.

He left, called Iris and got voicemail. Instead of leaving a message he drove the couple of blocks to her house.

No one answered his knock but the door was open so he pushed it open and yelled, "Hello?"

He heard the sounds of an electric saw coming from upstairs so he ran lightly up, checking swiftly to see that Iris wasn't in bed sick or something. She wasn't.

He ran up to the attic and found Jack Chance sawing lengths of lumber in some complicated fashion that seemed to make sense to him.

Since Geoff was challenged by pre-fab furniture he wasn't inclined to be critical. Not wanting to startle the man so he cut off his own leg or something, Geoff flicked the light switch. That got Jack's attention and with a wave he switched off the saw. That didn't help the noise level a whole lot since the Grateful Dead filled all the spaces the saw had left empty.

"I'm looking for Iris," he yelled.

"Huh?" Jack took an earplug out of his ear. Then, with another motion of his hand, went over and flipped off the boom box.

"Hi, Geoff, How are you?"

"Great. Looking for Iris."

"Oh, She's not here. Went to the hospital."

"The hospital?"

Jack scratched his head. Sawdust covered him the way icing sugar covered Iris's lemon bars. "Maybe not the hospital. A clinic?"

He felt alarm thud through him, couldn't get the picture out of his mind of her sucking on a thermometer the other day. Why hadn't he made her see a doctor then? "Is she sick? Is it serious?"

Jack looked both bemused and guilty. Like he'd said something he was going to get in trouble for. "I stay out of all that women's stuff. You'd better ask Daphne."

And then, with a friendly wave, he threw the music back on. By the time Geoff had hit the second stair on his way back down, the saw was roaring away again.

He should have asked Jack for Daphne's cell number, kicked himself for his stupidity, but couldn't face going through the process to get Jack's attention again. He jumped in his car and drove as fast as he could to Daphne and Jack's place, trying to convince himself that if anything was seriously wrong Jack wouldn't be sawing lengths of wood in Iris's attic.

He didn't bother to park in the big area they reserved for cars, but screeched to a halt in front of the house and jumped out. He was banging on the front door in seconds.

It seemed a century before Daphne opened the door and when she did she opened her eyes in surprise. "Why Geoff. Is everything all right?" She glanced behind him as though her barn might be on fire.

"I'm looking for Iris. Jack said she was in hospital."

She closed her eyes briefly in a move that clearly said, 'God give me patience.' "I do not know why I ever tell that man anything. Of course Iris isn't in hospital. She's gone for a routine medical procedure. Nothing alarming."

His heart rate started to slow, not so much because of Daphne's words but because he reasoned that if Iris was ill or hurt her mother would be at her side, not inside her house with her hands covered in rapidly drying clay. She wore an apron that was dusty with dried clay and she had a gray chunk of it stuck in her hair.

"Okay. Sorry I bothered you. I thought – when the creative writing circle was meeting without her, and then Jack said – well, I was worried."

Daphne smiled at him. "She's lucky to have someone to worry about her. Usually, Iris is always the one worrying about everybody else."

"Okay, I'd better get going."

"Would you like some tea or something?"

"No. I'll let you get back to your pottery."

She glanced down at herself as though she'd forgotten she was working with clay.

He couldn't settle. He knew that if something was wrong Daphne would have told him but then if it was some routine procedure, why hadn't Iris told him she was going? He'd seen her this morning.

He didn't like the feelings that started to swirl around inside him so he pulled on running gear and headed out. Ever since the day he'd got himself lost he always made sure he had his phone with its handy GPS and a bottle of water. But of course, since then he'd never become disoriented. He warmed up a little then ran six miles at an easy place. He was falling into routines and patterns. He jogged when he got home early enough. He worked out in the gym most mornings since he was up at the crack of dawn with Iris anyway.

He liked it here, he realized. He liked this small town with its natural beauty and old hippies. There was no place to buy men's clothes that he'd actually wear in this town but there were three crystal shops. Yoga wasn't served up with Pilates like he was used to. It was served with meditation.

He jogged home, did some stretches while he watched the evening news, took a shower.

When he came out of the shower he saw that Iris had called and he returned the call immediately, relief sluicing through him.

"Hi," she said, sounding the way she always did.

"Hi." He waited for her to tell him where she'd been but she didn't.

"I'm starving and I don't feel like cooking. Could I interest you in pizza or Thai?"

"Sure, I could do that."

She obviously heard hesitation. "Unless you want to head out of town and sit in an actual restaurant."

"No. Take-out's good. You want to come here or should I come to you?"

"I'm thinking of starting a fire. Why don't you come here?"

"I'll pick up the food on the way. Be there in thirty or forty."

He stood waiting for his order to be ready, thinking how quickly they'd fallen into routines. There'd been no need to go over the menu. They already knew what they'd order from the Thai restaurant, in the same way they both liked the fully loaded pizza. So how was it that they had the take-out restaurant intimacy down cold and yet she didn't want to share with him details of a medical procedure? Even if it was one of those girl things he didn't really want to know about, what was the big deal telling him she was going?

The more he contemplated that she hadn't told him what was going on the less he liked it.

When he got to her place she opened the door looking healthy and as though she'd freshened up. Her lips were freshly glossed and her hair just-brushed. "Hi," she said, leaning in for a kiss.

"Hi." He kissed her back until a rustle of the bag between them, and the pungent odor of Thai food brought them to their senses. "Come on through," she said and he followed her to the kitchen.

He waited for her to tell him about her appointment. She told him an amusing story about two five-year-olds she'd overheard at Sunflower discussing where babies came from.

He told her that after Rosalind complained yet again about Lear he'd finally told her that she could thank the bard for her own name. "Fair Rosalind," I told her, 'Is from As You Like It.'"

"Well, that's good. Maybe she'll have more respect for Shakespeare."

Except some comic genius went to the library at lunch time, or more likely online, and next thing you know, the boys are saying, "Where Virtue is no horn-maker; and my Rosalind is virtuous."

"Oh, dear."

"Yeah. That horn-maker never gets old."

"Boys found it funny in Shakespeare's time."

"And still do unfortunately for our fair Rosalind. For which I feel somewhat guilty."

"But not too guilty."

He shook his head.

"And how was your day?" he asked.

While she took plates out of the cupboard and set them on the counter, he flipped open all the lids on the take out.

"It was good. Now that we've got our impromptu writing group happening, I'm writing again. I have to thank you for that." She touched him briefly. "I don't know why I ever stopped."

"That's great," he said warmly. "In fact I stopped in today to share an idea with the group."

Her hands paused for a second as she reached for napkins. "Oh?"

"Yeah. You weren't there." He paused but she didn't speak. "Your dad tell you I came by?"

Now she turned to him surprise and a slight wariness in her expression. "You came here? To the house?"

"I was worried about you. Your dad said you were at the hospital so I got a lot more worried."

Her gaze dropped and a blush warmed her cheeks. "I wasn't at the hospital."

"So your mom said."

133

Her gaze flew back to his. "You went to my parents' house?"

"That's a funny thing. People say hospital and I worry. Call me crazy."

"What did my moth—"

He cut her off. "What's going on?" He edged closer, took her hands in his and looked into her eyes. "If there's some issue with your health I'd like to think I can help you in some way. I'm here for you."

For a second he saw longing in her eyes so fierce he wanted to kiss her and tell her everything was going to be okay. But how could he do that when he didn't know squat?

She squeezed his hands and took a step back. "I'm healthy. Very healthy, in fact."

"Okay."

She blew out a breath. "I did not plan on having to tell you this for a while." She fiddled with the take-out boxes. Rearranging them on the counter. She glanced at him and away again. "I—I'm thinking about having a baby."

"A baby." So not where he'd imagined this conversation going.

"When I went to the doctor for my annual check up she suggested that – for reasons I won't go into – I should move on it if I want to have kids. I've always known I wanted to be a mother."

"Move on it." He could feel his eyes squinting the way he got when one of his students was being a smart ass.

"Yes."

"What does move on it mean exactly?" He conducted a rapid review and knew they'd been using condoms scrupulously, though now he thought back to the first time her little hesitation made sense. She hadn't been having second thoughts about getting intimate with him. She'd contemplated using him for stud service.

"I've been looking at sperm donors."

"Sperm donors." He could not believe he was having this conversation like it was normal back and forth over Pad Thai.

"I mean from a sperm bank, of course."

"So you're buying sperm from strangers?"

"I have bought one lot so far yes. Well, technically my sister Rose bought it for me for a birthday present." And now he recalled her getting all emotional over her sister's birthday card. So all the family must know. Everyone in town, probably, but the guy who was actually sleeping with her.

He put his plate back on the counter, shoved the chop sticks into the center of the tangle of noodles and sauce. A chunk of nut bounced and tumbled onto the counter.

He felt so stunned he wasn't sure what to even say. The only time he'd felt remotely like this was when his wife dumped him by text.

For some weird reason this seemed worse.

"I guess I've got two obvious questions."

She nodded as though already answering them. "I know. I should have told you."

"Yep. There's that. And also, you're paying to have some stranger, some med student's seed stuffed up you while you've got a living guy right here that you're sleeping with. Did it occur to you to even ask me?"

"Of course it did." She pushed her barely touched plate to the counter too. "But, I hardly know you."

He laughed derisively. "You know me a hell of a lot better than the guy in vial B-4678."

"But that guy got paid to donate his seed. It's a business transaction, pure and simple. With you, it's so much more complicated."

"You could have asked me!"

"You are a married man."

"Technically."

"Legally!"

"I'm getting a divorce."

"But don't you see? You're not even free from your last woman. You're in no position to be thinking of anything permanent. So if you volunteered to father my child, I'd always know you were out there. And when you moved to another school or moved on from me and found another woman, you'd be the parent that baby always wondered about."

Chapter Sixteen

He took a step back, leaned against the kitchen counter. He tried to do the distancing thing he'd learned as a teacher. He couldn't get involved in his students' problems. His job was to listen and try to help the kids find solutions.

He was having a hell of a time trying to find a similar distance here, tonight. In fact, it couldn't be done. He was involved with this crazy stubborn woman. Involved up to his armpits.

He tried the oldest distancing trick in the book. Counted to ten.

If he didn't feel this rage of emotion it would be easier. He might be able to fish out one or two pertinent issues and hang onto them like conversational life preservers.

"You turned thirty-three a few weeks ago. What's the big rush?"

"I've got endometriosis. It's not a big deal except that it can interfere with fertility. My doctor said sooner rather than later."

"And we were going to go along having this relationship, this all condom all the time relationship, while you took your temperature and dashed off to some clinic to be artificially inseminated once a month."

"No."

He cocked an eyebrow at her.

"I hadn't thought it through, obviously."

She took a step closer to him. "This really has nothing to do with you."

He held a hand up to stop her from coming closer. "Oh, it does have something to do with me. It really, really does. What happens when you wind up pregnant and everyone in Hidden Falls thinks I'm the father?"

"We tell the truth."

"That you were cheating on me with a turkey baster?"

"Oh, come on. This thing we have is great. It's amazing, actually, but obviously it's a temporary thing."

"Why do you always say that?"

"Because you're still—you're not divorced yet. I'm a transition person. It will be a while before you're ready to settle down again."

"And you've decided this. Unilaterally."

"Everybody knows you don't end up with the first person you sleep with after you split up from a marriage."

"I don't believe this. Our future is being determined by some online quiz? Everybody knows? That's your authority?" His voice was rising, getting louder and it felt good. "Did you even think about asking me what I feel?"

He saw her looking confused and guilty and lost. "I—I guess I made some assumptions."

He shook his head. "I didn't think I'd be happy again. Not for a long time." He picked up his keys. Headed for the door. "And I was. Thank you for that."

"So that's it?" It was her turn to yell now. She followed him to the door. "You're leaving because I didn't tell you I was making a decision about my own body and my own future without consulting you?"

He turned. Tried to formulate a true answer. "That's part of it. But frankly, I don't have a lot of respect for what you're doing. It's selfish. It's messed up and, if you ask me, you don't want a relationship with an adult. You love to fix wounded children."

She folded her arms across her chest and glared at him. "Are you putting yourself in that category?"

"Oh, I was. I was one lost and wounded little boy when I first got my ass handed to me. But I'm not any more. You did help me heal. You made me realize that – and believe me it hurts me to say this – that my marriage wasn't as happy as I'd always pretended."

"What are you--?"

"I'm saying you made me happy. No. That's not true and I think it's what really scares you. You didn't make me happy any more than I made you happy. We were happy together."

"I—"

"Yeah. It's a risk. I'm a risky prospect, I can see that. The everybody knowses of the world would see a guy of thirty-five who's already failed at marriage once. They'd tell you to run a mile. Or to use me for sex and get yourself a designer kid that won't come with any baggage or anyone else in the world wanting a say in its life or its future."

"That is unfair on so many levels."

He ignored her interruption, continuing his theme. "But what if I am over my wife?"

"You couldn't be. You never talk about her."

A flicker of humor laced its way through the ice inside him. "Then let me talk about her now. Let me tell you something. She's moved in with my good buddy the lawyer."

She blinked at the sudden change of subject but soon caught up. "Already?"

One of the things he'd come to like, maybe even love, about Iris was how quickly she grasped the meaning behind people's words. Her eyes widened and she shook her head slowly. "Oh my gosh. You don't move in with someone you just started seeing. This must have been going on while you were married. I wonder how long?"

"Oh, my gosh isn't exactly how I phrased it but you got the gist of it. For who knows how long in my marriage, my best friend was banging my wife. Or I should say, ex best friend and ex-wife."

"I don't even know what to say. You must be devastated."

He looked at the keys in his hand. Silver keys to the car he'd driven away from LA in and the brand new apartment keys to his new living arrangement. "You know what's funny? I'm more devastated about losing you."

"But, wait, this isn't finished. You can't just—"

He opened the door. "Goodnight," he said, and shut it carefully behind him.

The door opened while he was walking toward his car. "Wait," she called. "Are you breaking up with me?"

He turned back. She was so pretty standing there, backlit, her eyes appearing huge in her shadowed face. "According to you, we were never together."

And he turned and kept walking. After a few moments he heard the snap as her door shut behind him like the sound of a fatal gunshot.

Chapter Seventeen

Geoff got through every day. He had places he needed to be, classes to teach, papers to grade, meetings to attend.

When Friday arrived, Tara Barnes sought him out. "Hey stranger," she said giving him her big friendly smile. "You coming for a drink tonight?"

He was about to refuse automatically but she put a hand on his arm. "Don't say no. It's my birthday. Help me celebrate?"

And he thought, what the hell? So he forced enthusiasm into his tone. "Yeah, why not?"

"Great. Ellen is driving us all in her van so we can have a couple of drinks if we want." She nudged her shoulder against him. "I plan to have a lot of fun tonight," she said, looking up at him in a way that could only be termed flirtatious.

"Great," he said again.

He bumped into Ellen in the teacher's lounge later that day while she was eating her lunch, a magazine open on her knee. "Hear you're driving the party bus," he said to her.

She glanced around to make sure no one was in earshot. The school nurse was talking with the Spanish teacher at a table on the other side of the room. She motioned him to come and sit beside her. "What's going on with you?"

"Nothing."

"I haven't taught high school for twenty years not to know when somebody's suffering."

He thought he'd been putting on such a good façade. Hell it fooled Tara enough that she was hitting on him. "What do you mean?"

She sighed. "Are you really going to make me do this? You look like hell, like you're not sleeping. Your socks don't match and you haven't shaved."

He felt like a teenager with a heartache. He glanced down and damn it, she was right. He had on one brown sock and one black sock. Hadn't even noticed. "I'm going to Tara's birthday party, aren't I?"

She settled a teacher's gaze on him, the kind that made you squirm even if you hadn't done anything wrong. "You're not planning to do something really stupid are you?"

"Define stupid," he said, thinking maybe he was.

She dropped her voice and leaned closer. "Tara Barnes makes no secret of the fact that she'd like to jump your very fine bones."

"You said I look like hell."

"Everything's relative," she said with a sardonic look. "Around here, you're still the best looking guy we've seen in a long time. And she has her eye on you."

"So?"

"So I don't think you're interested and if you two get involved and it doesn't work out, the last thing we need is drama among the teaching staff." She shuddered and he suspected she was speaking from experience. "So I'm telling you as a friend and a fellow teacher that you should think very carefully before getting involved with a colleague."

Sometimes he was more clueless than the most naïve freshman. "You're right. I've always steered clear of getting involved with other teachers."

"I know it can be hard to resist. We see each other every day. And she is very attractive."

He considered the issue of attraction for a moment and knew that for him there was only one woman in Hidden Falls. "She's hot all right. But I'm not interested."

She nodded, looking a lot more sympathetic now he'd told her he wouldn't be causing inter-staff drama. "Still hurting over your wife?"

Irritation stabbed at him. "Why does everyone assume that?"

"Because you're in the middle of a divorce. Seems like a reasonable assumption."

"Well, my ex-wife is not the reason I'm not interested in Tara." A second of silence passed and he felt the disbelief coming off Ellen. He said, "I'm in love with somebody else." He felt the shock go through him as he said the words, said them so fluidly and easily that he realized he'd known on some level for a while now that he was crazy in love with Iris.

"In love with someone else?"

"I know it sounds crazy, but it's true."

"Then why are you so miserable?"

"Because she, like everyone else, thinks I'm not ready for a relationship. But I am."

"You're sure? Have you considered that this might be a rebound relationship?"

"Yes. Of course I've considered that. But this isn't a rebound. I love her in a way I've never loved a woman before. And she doesn't believe me."

"You can't exactly blame the woman."

"How do I let her know that I'm not rebounding? That I love her?" This was the question that haunted him at night and messed with his concentration during the day.

"I don't know."

He wanted to kick something. He knew he had to act a little more mature than his students even though he didn't feel it. He scowled instead. "Iris Chance is one stubborn woman who only hears what she wants to hear."

Ellen was in the act of resealing the plastic container her lunch had come in but her hands stilled and she glanced up at him. "Iris Chance? You're in love with Iris?"

"Yeah." He'd forgotten once again that in a town this size most everyone knew everyone. Of course Ellen knew Iris. "You know her."

"She owns the best coffee shop in town. In fact, I'm probably the reason you two met. I sent you to Sunflower when you first moved here. Remember?"

"Yeah. I do. And I should thank you for that except that she kicked my ass out of her life."

The other English teacher stared at him but almost through him, like she was looking at something else. "She came to a couple of parent teacher interviews. You get to see another side of a person when they come to parent teacher interviews."

"What?" He wondered if they were talking about the same person. "Iris doesn't have kids."

"No. But the man she was dating at the time did. Rob Granger. His son was doing some foolish things. Mostly, I think, because he was upset about his parents' break-up."

He'd heard about Rob. The last guy Iris had dated. She'd never mentioned he'd had kids or that it had been serious enough that she attended parent teacher conferences. "What happened?"

"Rob went back to his wife. Back to his family. They moved away after that. I think they're in Seattle now."

If a thunderbolt had streaked down from the sky shouting out a message, it couldn't have been clearer. "Iris's last boyfriend went back to his ex-wife?" So many things started to make sense. "Oh, that's perfect."

She made a sympathetic face. "Bad luck for you I'm afraid."

"No wonder she can't believe I'm truly free." And how on earth did he show her he was?

At Ellen's raised eyebrows he said, "Okay, not truly free. Not all the way free, but emotionally free which is the important thing."

"If there's anything I can do to help, ask."

"Wow. That's so nice of you. You must believe in me and Iris as a couple."

She picked up her reusable sandwich bag, slipped in the plastic tub and the fork she'd brought from home and tucked it tidily away. "I believe in you and anyone who doesn't work at this school."

As she walked away, he thought, this is a woman who's been married a long time. He said, "Hey, what makes a woman really believe a man loves her?" The nurse and the Spanish teacher stopped their conversation to stare at him. He didn't even care that he was baring his soul to strangers.

Ellen paused, turned back. "The grand gesture. Every woman secretly yearns for a man to slay a dragon, swim through a river of crocodiles to get to her, to prove his love."

"Si," the Spanish teacher agreed.

"Not a lot of dragons or crocodiles in Hidden Falls," he said. "But thanks."

"Don't be so literal," Ellen chided like he was a remedial student in her English class.

He thought rapidly, assessed and discarded a dozen foolish ideas. Then he had it. The answer was so simple. "Could a grand gesture be a signature on a piece of paper?"

"You're writing her a letter?" She did not look impressed with his heroic possibilities. The school nurse shook her head.

"No. I was thinking a judge's signature on a divorce decree."

Ellen smiled at him. "Now you're getting somewhere."

He was so relieved he walked right over, grabbed her and kissed her cheek.

Ellen laughed, but she blushed a little too. She patted him on the shoulder. "Plus you're gorgeous which will definitely help."

He put in the call to his lawyer immediately, since he had no secrets from the two other women who had resumed their conversation. But his lawyer was in a meeting and he had to leave a message. Then, since he couldn't break the rules he imposed on his students, he turned off his cell phone and went to class.

He'd planned to skip the after work drink but it was soon clear that nearly all the teachers were going since it was Tara's birthday. Her thirtieth, it turned out. He made a point of sitting across the table and down a few from the birthday girl and making conversation with one of the biology teachers, a guy a little older than him who was happy to talk sports.

He was sipping a beer, wondering how soon he could get away, when the lawyer called back. He excused himself from the crowded, noisy table and stepped outside. Rain drizzled down and he huddled under the awning.

"What can I do for you?" his lawyer asked. She was a no-nonsense type who had told him up front she wasn't interested in drama or blame. "Keep that for the therapist's office. I am a negotiator. I will get you the best deal I can within the law. How does that sound?" He'd thought it sounded fine. Signed up with her, sent her all the documentation and listings of every cent of assets he and his wife owned together and those that he owned separately. Then months had dribbled by with little contact.

"I need my divorce now," Geoff said to his lawyer, watching water drip off the awning and into a puddle.

"These things take time, Geoff."

"I don't have time. The law says we can get divorced in California if we've lived apart for six months. It's been six and a half months."

"Right. But you've got assets to divide and—"

"Get hold of her lawyer. Find out what she wants. Let's meet and get this thing done."

"You don't want to come across as too eager. If they sense weakness—"

"I don't care. I am eager. If we're both willing to be reasonable we can settle this thing in an afternoon."

She argued a little longer and he heard her out, then he said, "I've got no classes next Friday. I'll drive down Thursday night. I can meet anytime Friday. I want an agreement by the end of the day. Let's do this."

"I'll do my best to set something up. I'll get back to you."

He began to feel better. If he could prove to Iris that there was no possibility he was going back to his wife then maybe she'd give this thing with them a chance. Maybe he wasn't ready for kids right this second, but he thought he'd be a good father.

As he headed back into the restaurant, he thought, No, that wasn't it and he knew it. He needed to prove to Iris that he was in love with her, forever and ever love.

But the divorce was a good start.

Chapter Eighteen

Iris hated herself for dressing with extra care in the mornings and making sure she was out front serving every customer. But all the lipstick and hair products didn't lure Geoff into Sunflower.

Nothing lured him in.

He didn't come for his morning coffee and muffin. He broke the daily routine he'd formed from the first day he'd come in here with an order for his first staff meeting.

The morning after their argument, she made excuses for him. The second day, she rehearsed what she'd say, how natural she'd act. If they could get back to an easy customer/coffee shop owner friendship, then maybe she wouldn't feel so empty and frustrated, as though they were in the middle of an argument and the other person had slipped away to the washroom and never come back.

She had things to say. Things she wanted him to understand. He'd been completely out of line to try and make her feel guilty. He needed to understand that.

But how did she get him to see his mistake if she couldn't even talk to him?

She was staring longingly at the door, willing it to open and Geoff to walk in when Dosana walked up behind her. Iris saw her glance at the door and then back at Iris. Quickly, she reverted her attention to tidying up the china cups.

"Haven't seen Geoff in a few days," Dosana said, without quite putting a question mark at the end although it was clearly implied.

"No. Maybe he's making coffee at home now."

"And baking his own delicious muffins?"

She didn't answer. She was conscious of an ache somewhere in the region of her solar plexus. She wanted to lean on Dosana's tattooed shoulder and cry, but that wasn't going to solve her problems or bring Geoff back.

Dosana patted her. "If you want to talk about anything, I'm always here."

"Thanks."

"I mean it."

Iris wasn't good at talking about her problems. She was so much better with other people's problems. As Dosana turned to grab a cloth and go wipe the tables, she said, "He plays hide and seek with a cat."

"What?" Dosana looked at her as though maybe she hadn't heard right.

"There's this cat that lives in Geoff's building. It hangs out at his place sometimes. They play hide and seek."

"Insane, but adorable." The red streak in her hair had faded to a muted cherry. "And not why you have black circles under your eyes and tragedy weighing down your shoulders."

"He found out that I'm planning to have a child on my own. He didn't take it so well."

"Ah. Did you really think he was going to?"

"I didn't think it was any of his business. I still don't."

"I'm guessing he has a different opinion."

"Yeah."

"Damn. What are you going to do?"

"I'm going to have my baby. It would have been nice to have Geoff around for a while longer but it was never going to work out long term. I'm a realist. So, a bit of heartache now beats a whole lot more heartache later."

"I liked you two together."

She pushed cups and saucers around like chess pieces. "Were we really together?"

"Seemed like you were only apart when you guys were at work. Call me crazy. Sure seemed like you were together."

Geoff usually considered himself a pretty laid back guy. Easy going even so it was strange to feel this burning compulsion to get his divorce. To be free.

So he pushed his lawyer a little harder. Got his meeting.

And then he packed up his car and, much sooner than he'd imagined, found himself making the drive back to LA.

It was strange driving back down I-5 and then onto 101 recalling his very different feelings when he'd driven up to Hidden Falls only five months ago.

He'd still been angry then, hurting, in shock that his marriage had ended with the sudden jolt of a text message out of the blue.

But now that time had passed, he could see what he hadn't been able to see before. The marriage hadn't been working.

Could it have been saved?

He watched the trees spin by and the sun move slowly across the sky as he followed the road mile after mile. Summer was on its way and his first truncated year at Jefferson High was almost over. When he stopped to grab a coffee, he stood outside in the warmth of early June sunshine and stretched his cramped muscles. He had a lot of time to think.

Yes, he thought. The marriage could have been saved. In spite of the way she'd acted recently, he thought he and Brianna were both essentially decent people. They'd managed to live together for a few years in reasonable harmony. He'd imagined that was enough.

But it hadn't been enough for his wife.

While he didn't respect her methods of ending the marriage he had a sneaking sympathy for her. How difficult it must have been to try and end something that wasn't particularly bad. It simply wasn't very good.

At the time he'd felt black and angry, as the life he'd known had blown up in his face. What he couldn't have foreseen at the time was that even if her methods sucked, Bri's instincts to end the marriage were right.

If she hadn't dumped his ass, he never would have met Iris.

He sipped coffee and got back behind the wheel for another grueling stint of road travel. Iris wasn't easy. Life with her would never be polite and reasonably harmonious. She was passionate, creative, a nurturer who didn't know how to nurture herself.

She made him laugh, she made him angry, she made him feel. He loved her with all his heart and he knew that she was scared enough, stubborn enough that she'd believe her own foolish fear rather than open up to the truth that could end up hurting her.

He might not be a brilliant writer like she was but he was a man who loved and understood story. Ellen had been right. Iris needed the grand gesture, the dragon slain for her.

There weren't many dragons lurking in the Pacific Northwest but he was fairly certain there was some kind of demon hiding within Iris that made her fearful of believing a recently separated man could love again so quickly.

He knew it was possible because he was that man.

So, the dragon he had to slay was the fear inside Iris.

His grand gesture might not be the stuff of legend and fable, but it was a pretty big deal for him.

He was going to give Iris his freedom.

And hope very much she took it back from him again.

Geoff walked into the familiar offices of his former best friend Stephen J. Parker, as it said on the door. He thought of all the times he'd dropped by here to pick up his buddy for a run after work, or to grab a beer.

He'd never imagined he'd enter the offices of Stephen Jasper (and how many people even knew Steve's middle name?) as a client – not of his former best friend – but of a lawyer who'd been recommended to him. And that his former best friend would be representing Geoff's wife. Now his girlfriend.

He'd met with his own lawyer that morning and drilled into her once more that he wanted the details finalized today. Sixteen hours on the road with a couple of hours snatched sleep had not mellowed him.

"I'd have told you that you were crazy," she said, "that they'd use your haste against you. But I think they might be in a hurry too."

"What do you mean?"

"I think they both feel guilty, frankly. The sooner you're divorced and they can forget what they did to you the happier they'll be."

He nodded. He knew both of them well enough that he thought his lawyer might be right. "Good," he said briskly. "Let's do this thing."

"I have to warn you, even though it must kill you to see your ex-wife and your ex-friend together in the same room, negotiating the end of your marriage, you can't lose your cool."

He nodded briskly but she wasn't finished. "Promise me. No yelling. No accusations. For God's sake, no threats. Keep your understandable anger for your therapist. Got it?"

"I don't think you have to worry," he said.

Her gaze sharpened and he felt she was searching his face. "Okay," she said at last. "You'll do."

So he found himself walking into the conference room with a sense of unreality. His exes were both already there. Both glanced up at him with similar guilty expressions on their faces. They had note pads in front of them. On Steve's some notes were already scribbled in handwriting almost as familiar to Geoff as his own.

For a hideous moment no one moved or spoke.

Then his attorney stepped past him. She seld out her hand to Steve. "I'm Edna Silver, we spoke on the phone."

That broke the ice. He stepped forward behind her thinking, what the hell? He could be the bigger man. He held out his hand to his former friend first. As they shook he felt a sadness go through him. He thought of all the times they'd laughed together, hit some kind of a ball around a court together, talked about their futures. They'd shared details, like the financial assets even now listed on printouts for today's discussion.

"Good to see you," Steve managed.

He nodded.

He turned finally to the woman he'd been married to for six years. She looked good, he thought. She'd colored her hair and something about her clothes seemed different. Tighter, more stylish. He thought she'd lost weight.

"How are you Brianna?" he said. He couldn't shake her hand, that was stupid. Kiss her cheek? He didn't think so. So he stood there looking at her, not touching.

She said, "I'm okay." She looked stubborn and unapproachable but he'd known her for long enough that he recognized she felt guilty and didn't know how to apologize.

He realized he didn't need her to.

Once more he acknowledged a sadness. Once he'd planned to spend the rest of his life with this woman. Now he'd probably never see her again once this meeting was over. Why would they? They had no kids, nothing to tie them, their families had always been cordial but never particularly close.

His lawyer sat down and he settled beside her.

She pulled a stack of printed pages from her briefcase and gave each person one. "This is my client's settlement offer. We believe it's more than fair. As Geoff has come a considerable way in order to attend this meeting, I suggest we do our best to come to an agreement today."

"Yes, so do we. I mean, my client agrees." His former friend said.

And in less than an hour, the agreement was reached. Bloodless, emotionless, the end of a marriage came down to valuing assets and splitting them fairly.

When he left, he turned back to his almost ex wife. This time he kissed her cheek. "I hope you'll be happy."

"You too," she said.

And maybe that was as much as they could hope for.

He took the signed agreement, that now only needed to be ratified by a judge, a formality that would officially end the marriage.

He spent the rest of Friday and all of Saturday getting rid of the rest of his stuff. He knew with certainty that he wouldn't ever live in this city again. As he donated the last box to Goodwill he felt a chapter of his life ending.

When he climbed into his car and headed out of LA that evening, he no longer felt as though he were leaving. This time, he was heading toward a woman who held his heart in her bread-kneading, barista hands.

He couldn't wait to give it to her.

Chapter Nineteen

By Saturday Iris couldn't stand it anymore. She and Geoff had parted without any kind of resolution. She missed seeing him in the mornings when he dropped in for his morning coffee looking sleepy and sexy. Usually, they'd woken up together a couple of hours earlier. He'd walk in through the door and she'd glance up and catch him looking at her and warmth would whoosh through her hard and fast.

Now it seemed she grew more wistful with each ring of those foolish bells that ushered in a customer who wasn't Geoff.

Sunday was her usual day off but with Milo and two other high school students working today plus Dosana to supervise she felt she could take a couple of hours off. She'd go and see Geoff she decided, simply talk to him.

Maybe she couldn't have back what she'd had before but she didn't want to live in a town this small with a man who harbored hard feelings against her.

"I'm going out for a couple of hours," she told Dosana.

"Okay." Dosana didn't comment, not even when she grabbed an Americano to go and slipped two of Geoff's favorite muffins into a bag.

She took off her apron and hung it up in the back. Then she headed out. She needed to pick up her car at her place since she'd walked to work. But once there she decided to brush her teeth and redo her makeup, change into her new jeans and a flattering shirt she'd bought in Portland.

She brushed her long hair until it shone.

She even patted the Alice Munro book he'd given her for good luck.

With a heartrate definitely elevated she pulled up in front of Geoff's apartment. She sat in her car staring at the front door as though she could will him to appear. Since her conjuring skills hadn't improved since she'd tried to make him walk into Sunflower every day for the past week, she decided to call him.

But he didn't pick up.

Typical. Why couldn't he at least be man enough to talk to her? She got out of the car and stalked to the front door of his building. It was supposed to be secure but half the time the door was propped open so that guests could come and go and the apartment cats could wander at will.

The door was propped open now and she walked in. She ran lightly up to Geoff's apartment picturing him marking papers or attempting to make coffee half as good as what she served in Sunflower.

She balanced the coffee and the bag of muffins in one hand as she banged on his door with the other.

Nothing.

She waited a moment and then knocked again.

A small furry body butted against her legs and she looked down to see Cat clearly as anxious as she was to see Geoff.

"Where is he?" she asked the cat who seemed to be looking at her with the same question in his eyes.

A woman emerged from an apartment down the hall. They'd seen each other a few times. She nodded. "Is the cat bothering you?"

"Oh, is he yours? No. He's sweet."

"He's got a big man crush on Geoff that's for sure. He sure misses him when he's gone."

"Geoff's gone?"

"Sure. I thought you knew. He went to LA for the weekend."

"LA?" She couldn't help the shock in her voice. Her entire system was shocked. "You're sure it was LA?" LA where he'd come from? Where his wife lived?

"Yeah." The woman looked sorry to have delivered bad news. "Pretty sure."

She bent down to pat the cat, hoping to hide the wave of hurt she felt washing over her. She knew she had the kind of face that showed all her emotions and she didn't particularly want this virtual stranger to witness her distress.

"Did you want me to give him a message or anything?"

"No. It's fine. I forgot he was going away this weekend," she said as casually as she could manage. "I'll catch him when he's back."

"Okay."

She rose. "I'll see you soon, little cat."

And she turned and headed for the door, sipping the coffee so Geoff's neighbor wouldn't think she was the kind of pathetic woman who brought coffee to a man who had gone home to his wife.

She couldn't go back to work. She called Dosana and made sure the younger woman could close.

"Yeah. Sure. No problem."

"Everything okay?" she asked.

"Yep. It's quiet. Milo's trying out some of his poetry on that Goth girl waif who adores him."

"Oh, that's so cute," she said in spite of her misery.

"You okay? You sound kind of funny."

"I'm fine." She glanced at her watch. "My dad's probably working on my house now. I might go supervise."

"I thought… Never mind. If you need anything, you know I'm here for you."

"Yeah. Thanks. See you tomorrow."

When she let herself into the house the sound of heavy metal was as comforting as a hug. And boy, could she use a hug.

"Dad!" she yelled, banging up the stairs. She stopped, knowing he couldn't hear her anyway and dashed into her bedroom where she stripped out of her seduce the local high school English teacher clothes and shoved herself into a faded old pair of jeans and an ancient T-shirt that she kept for doing disgusting jobs.

She pushed her feet into sneakers and tied her hair out of the way. That done, she headed up to the third floor once more.

Jack Chance was bobbing his head in time to "Highway to Hell" as he nailed together the cubbies for her book and toy shelves.

A wave of affection rolled through her as she thought about how lucky she'd been to have been brought up by Jack and Daphne and not her hopeless biological parents.

She got his attention by waving at him and he gave her his big smile. She turned the music down to human volume and walked over to him. "Hey, Dad, how's it going up here?"

"Okay. I had a tiny bit of trouble fitting the first cube together but I think I figured it out."

"AC/DC always helps a person think clearly."

He grinned at her, doing the head banging thing and she suddenly had a mental image of him as a young guy in the 70s. In his element.

"Dad, I need a job. Something sweaty and muscular. I've got some stress I need to work out."

"I'm thrilled to have an extra pair of hands." He glanced around. "Tell you what, you can sand the edges of the fresh cuts."

She liked that he didn't pry or offer platitudes or do anything but what she'd asked him to do. Give her a job.

They worked for a while companionably. Hand sanding was a genius way to let off some of her hurt and anger and frustration. AC/DC gave way to the Stones on the boom box. She worked out the worst of her frustration, then, when her arm was sore and her throat dry, yelled, "Want some coffee?"

He nodded.

She ran downstairs, made a pot and added a few of her lemon bars straight out of the freezer. She'd taken to keeping them there so she didn't eat so many but all that happened was she discovered they were delicious frozen. Little lemon pastry Popsicles. She knew Jack felt the same way.

She poured coffee into two of her mother's coffee mugs that she most hoped would get broken and hiked it all up to the construction zone.

As though knowing she was ready to talk, Jack turned the volume of the music down farther and they settled side by side on the floor each holding a coffee, the treats between them on the plate.

There was relative silence for a moment as they both sipped coffee and Jack polished off a frozen lemon bar. "You have a talent with baking," he said, "that is for sure." As

161

though feeling that might have been unfeminist, and Jack prided himself on being strongly feminist, he added, "And you're a fine businesswoman."

However, today she didn't feel like a feminist or a businesswoman. She felt like a woman hurting because of a man. "Dad?"

"Mmm?" He was eyeing the lemon squares as his fingers hovered over the plate waiting for his brain to choose which pastry to pick up.

"Why do men betray women?"

Jack turned to her, paused in his lemon bar selection, and said, "You speaking in general or specific terms?"

"Both, I guess."

Jack didn't rush to speak. He took a moment to think about her question. "I imagine every situation is different."

"It's how you and Mom got together. She was betrayed by a man she trusted. Her professor." Jack and Daphne had never shielded their children from the truth. When Jack had met Daphne she was pregnant with another man's child. She'd fallen in love with her American History professor at university who was married and already had three children. She'd been a penniless young student but determined to have and raise her child. Jack had met and fallen for the young Daphne, partly because he admired her resolve. As a boy who'd been bounced around the foster system he was determined to help kids who had so few choices in their lives.

Their son, Ben, looked a lot like his African American father but Jack had been his real father just as he'd been the real father to all the Chance kids, the ones he and Daphne conceived and the ones they adopted.

"You're right. That man not only betrayed Daphne, he betrayed the university standards, his family and his conscience. But he also gave your mother and me a precious gift. Sometimes that's what happens. A betrayal can also be a gift."

"You got another gift when my birth father betrayed my birth mother." She heard the bitterness in her tone and realized the argument with Geoff had pulled up some bad memories for her.

Jack studied the lumpy troll coffee mug in his hands. "Not to be too critical of your birth mother but I think they betrayed each other. She got pregnant hoping that would make him leave his family. He thought he could have an affair with no consequences."

"That sure didn't work."

"No, sweetheart it didn't. And I would personally like to ram this sander down his throat for the way he treated you when you met him."

"Thanks, Dad." That still hurt when she thought about how eager she'd been to meet her 'real' father only to discover he preferred to pretend she didn't exist.

Jack gestured to the half finished space that would house her office and a playroom for the child she hoped to have soon. "Is this what's got you thinking about men and betrayal?"

"No. I'm – Dad, I think Geoff went back to his wife."

Jack's brows rose. "Geoff? But he's crazy about you."

"He was," she said miserably. "But then he found out about my plan to have a child on my own and he wasn't too thrilled about it."

Jack turned and looked at her. "Couldn't expect him to be."

"You took on a pregnant woman," she reminded him.

"But she didn't go get pregnant while I was seeing her."

She put her hands over her eyes. "Why does it have to be so complicated? I want a child. My doctor says I should do it soon. Then Geoff comes along. I like him. He likes me. But he's still married and there is no way he's ready for a serious relationship so soon. So I continue with my plan to have a child on my own. I don't understand why that's so bad. Wouldn't it be worse if I used Geoff to get pregnant?"

"I think using people is always wrong."

She shot him a glance. When her dad made cryptic utterances he was usually trying to get across an important message. "You think I was using him?"

"I don't know. Were you?"

"For affection? Companionship? Sex? Isn't that what people do in a relationship?" She pushed her feet out in front of her, straight ahead so she could see the tips of her sneakers. "Anyway, I drove him straight back to his wife." She scowled. "Which seems to be my specialty."

Jack reached over to pat her knee. "Know what I think?"

"That I'm a terrible person?"

"Iris, you are one of the best people I know. But sometimes you jump to conclusions before you have all the information."

"Why did he go to LA then? After he found out about my plan to get pregnant with a donor we had words. I haven't seen him since. He doesn't come into the café anymore. Today I went to his place and his neighbor said he's in LA where his wife lives. So, maybe she changed her mind."

"Maybe she did. Doesn't mean he went back to her."

"Why else would he drive hundreds of miles?"

Jack put the lumpen troll mug on the floor then used his free hands to enumerate. The forefinger of his right hand hit

164

the tip of the forefinger of his left. "He could be moving some more of his possessions." He banged the tip of his middle finger. "He could have an event he needs to attend." Ring finger, where the silver hippy ring announced to the world that he belonged to Daphne. "He could be going to tell her that he's not coming back." Finally, he held out both hands. "And you're right, he could be going to try and patch things up with her. I don't know. But neither do you. So, before you accuse him of betraying you, maybe you should check your facts."

"Doesn't matter anyway. He made it clear he doesn't want anything to do with me."

"He was probably pretty hurt. I think I would be in his situation."

"I guess I didn't handle things very well. I told myself it was none of his business what I did with my body."

"Relationships are never easy."

"It seems like they are for some people. I always end up feeling like I was second best."

"You are not ever second best," he sounded angry. "Do you hear me?"

"You're my dad. You have to say that."

"I've known you almost your whole life. I've watched you and I've loved you and I've suffered with you. You are the best."

She smiled feeling better because she knew how much Jack did believe in her, in all his kids. "You remember when Rob went back to his wife?"

"Of course I do. He broke your heart."

She shook her head. "The funny thing is he didn't. It hurt a lot but I think he did the right thing. Their break-up was caused by the stress of her mother dying, and some money issues. And it was so hard on the kids. He didn't love me and I didn't love him." When she turned to look at Jack she knew that he already sensed what she was about to say. "With Geoff? I feel like my heart is broken."

"Baby girl, sometimes you have to be clear about what you want and once you are, you have to fight for it."

She glanced around at the space she was creating with a future family in mind. "So do I give up my dream of a child?"

Once more her dad reached out and gave her knee a pat. "Patience has never been your strong suit."

She loved her dad, she really did, and as men went he was liberal and easy to talk to but there was no way she was going to discuss the intricacies of endometriosis with the man. Instead, she nodded. Then, she pushed back up to her feet.

"Okay," she said. "This attic isn't going to renovate itself."

He gulped back the last of his coffee. "As I was saying," and they both laughed.

Maybe her dad couldn't solve her problems for her now that she was grown, but he was here, helping her prepare her house for the next stage in her life.

Chapter Twenty

The next stage in her life. A flutter of unease disturbed her as she cleaned her house on Sunday. There was extra dust from the renovation project upstairs and she felt like she needed to keep busy.

Her temperature had gone up this morning. Her hand drifted to her middle where that flutter of unease batted wings with the thrill of the possibility that she'd have a child within the year.

Even though she now understood that choosing having a child on her own meant not continuing with Geoff she felt the urge to have a child of her own as strong in her as ever.

Some people dreamed of making music, or becoming a doctor or any of a million childhood dreams. In a household that prided itself on feminism, she'd grown up loving to play mother to a host of dolls, then to her brothers and sisters. If that wasn't enough to make Daphne shake her head, Iris's other passion was cooking.

She thought that standing barefoot and pregnant in a kitchen would be heaven.

When she woke the next morning her temperature was still elevated. And so was her combination of anxiety and excitement.

Monday dawned with the kind of sunrise that seemed sent from heaven as a sign. She stood in the early morning, drinking a cup of coffee and staring at the glorious sky. She had a moment's longing. How many mornings had Geoff stumbled out of bed much earlier than he had to so they could share this early time together?

Not even that many. A couple of months' worth of mornings. She understood that every time you chose a path you abandoned the one going in another direction. She sipped coffee as dawn bloomed.

If she went ahead and got pregnant on her own then she and Geoff didn't have a hope. But if she abandoned the baby path, or postponed it, then what? Great, maybe she and Geoff patched things up and carried on. But what were the chances he was going to be ready for kids? When they'd had their last argument he very clearly hadn't offered to step into the role of baby daddy.

He'd been pissed that she hadn't asked him to father her child, which spoke of ego, but he hadn't even hinted that he'd consider doing it.

She rinsed out her coffee cup and resolutely made the phone call to set up her insemination procedure. She'd do it after work so she could come straight back home and lie down.

Sure, she'd read that it didn't make a difference after the first fifteen minutes or so if you lay in bed or went cage fighting. But she didn't care. She was coming home to lie down with her feet up. She'd give every sperm a chance, even the lazy ones with a bad sense of direction.

"What is wrong with you?" Dosana snapped around eleven that morning.

"Hmm?"

"You have been staring into the fridge for the past five minutes. First, it's freezing in here and second we need to get ready for the lunch rush."

"I'm sorry." She snapped to attention, grabbed the butter she'd come for and closed the fridge door. Dosana was giving her a look that suggested she might be checking her for fever in a second. She stepped closer. "My temperature spiked."

"You mean?"

"I'm ovulating!" She danced around in a circle, the butter still in her hand.

"So you're going through with it?"

"My appointment with the clinic is at four o'clock today."

"Wow. This is intense." Dosana's eyes glowed and Iris felt her own excitement hike up a notch. "How do you feel?"

"Scared. Excited. Hopeful. Trying not to get my hopes up too high because, you know, it can take several tries."

Her assistant nodded. "But I know you. Once you get started, you'll keep going until there's a little Iris."

"Probably."

"This is so cool. If you need to head out early or anything, I can cover."

"No. It's fine. I'll work until around three-thirty and then head out."

"What about tomorrow? Do you need to stay in bed doing a headstand or something?"

She grinned. "It won't help. Tomorrow I'll be back here."

"How long until you know whether it worked or not?"

"A couple of weeks."

"I am not sure I can stand watching you zone out at the fridge door for two more weeks."

She chuckled. "I'll try really hard to act cool."

"And don't freak out if it doesn't work the first time. You gotta promise me."

"Do my best."

Dosana gave her a quick hug. "Kay. Um, listen, while you're in a good mood, can I talk to you about something?"

Panic flooded her. She grabbed Dosana's arm. "No. You can't quit. Absolutely not."

The younger woman looked startled. "So not what I wanted to talk about." She pushed her short hair back with the heel of her hand. "It's about my personal life."

"Okay." Please let it not be something awful.

"I'm seeing someone."

"That's great." She was so relieved.

Dosana took the butter out of Iris's hand and put it on the work bench. "It's Scott Beatty," she said in a rush.

Iris blinked at her. "You and Scott Beatty?" But now she thought about it, he'd taken to talking to Dosana when he came in and she'd been so relieved. "Wow."

"Are you okay with it? You said you weren't interested in him, but now that you and Geoff, um, I mean, if you liked him –"

"Oh, no. No. Really. I think you two would be perfect together. He's a nice guy."

"He is." Her assistant's smile suggested that more than 'nice' was going through her mind.

"But what about the—you know?"

"Kinky sex?"

She nodded.

Dosana twinkled at her. "Let's just say, he has forgotten all about his ex."

Iris probably would have asked questions she'd later regret getting the answers to but luckily the bell rang. "Better get back out front," Dosana said and she was gone.

For the rest of the day Iris tried extra hard not to act like a fool. It was ridiculous. There'd been a moment this morning when she'd thought that if Geoff came in before heading to school that she'd wait a cycle. At least long enough for them to have a conversation.

But she was glad he hadn't come in. She didn't want to be distracted by a guy who could only ever be temporary. She was a grown up with specific goals. Some sleepy eyed, sexy as hell schoolteacher was not going to change her game plan.

No matter how much she missed him.

Geoff woke up Monday morning still feeling like he was on a highway. He'd driven from LA straight through to Hidden Falls, a drive which was smooth apart from one accident that halted traffic for a half hour and a couple of mysterious slow downs where traffic crawled for a while for no reason he could see and then went back to normal speeds. He'd driven the entire trip in a day, which was foolish. The drive alone was fifteen hours. Add in a couple of meals and stretch breaks and he'd been sixteen hours on the road. Didn't get to his place until two and had to teach in the morning.

Never again, he swore to himself as he brushed his teeth. Then grinned at himself in the mirror. Never again was right. He had no need to go back to LA.

He was free.

Excitement churned in his belly. This was the day he laid it all on the line for Iris. He felt absurdly anxious, like if he didn't run right over there he'd be too late.

He was feeling crazy from lack of sleep, he knew. For a second he considered dropping in for his coffee and muffin on the way to school but he was already running late. He looked like shit from lack of sleep and too many hours driving. Besides, there wouldn't be time to talk.

No. He'd go by after school.

As he scraped a razor across his chin he wondered if flowers would be too much.

He got to school and discovered that his students had all clearly made a pact with each other over the weekend to drive him crazy. They'd 'forgotten' to do their homework or sat looking at him blankly when he asked a question in class. Even his creative writing students acted like they had better places to be.

He felt like yelling to them that he had places he'd rather be, too!

By the time the final bell rang, releasing him and his students from the frustration of facing each other, he couldn't get away fast enough.

He recognized the feeling now as simple excitement. He was crazy in love with Iris. He couldn't waste a moment letting her know that.

Stopping for flowers would take ten minutes and he suddenly felt that he didn't have ten extra minutes. He didn't have ten extra seconds to waste before telling her how he felt and pulling her into his arms. Once she believed that, and if she returned his sentiments, which he had to believe she did, then everything else was details.

When he got to Sunflower he felt the urgency return. He jumped out of his car, strode to the door and when he opened it the cascade of metal sunflowers jingled merrily as though welcoming him back.

He stepped through the doorway, his heart already thumping, and didn't immediately see Iris as he'd hoped. The younger girl with the crazy hair was there. Dosana he remembered in a flash.

When she saw him her eyes went wide.

"Hi Dosana," he said, wondering why she'd looked at him as though he were either a ghost or a serial killer.

"H-hi, ah, Geoff." She turned to rattle the big assed barista machine. "What can I get you?"

"Nothing right now. Is Iris in the back?" He hoped she'd hear his voice and come out.

"No. No. She's not here." She emptied wet grounds out of the coffee ground holder thing with a bang, her back to him.

His plan couldn't be unraveling already. "But she's always here."

"She had an appointment." She turned, still not looking at him and a really bad feeling stole over him like a cloud obscuring the sun.

"What kind of appointment?" They were the only two in the place but still he lowered his voice.

She met his gaze and then dropped hers again. "I can't tell you. I'm sorry."

"Tell me she's not following that stupid plan of hers?"

Dosana didn't answer and how could she, anyway. He was mostly talking to himself. He felt so much anger and disappointment he could barely see straight.

"Couldn't she at least have waited until we talked?"

"Maybe she thought you weren't into talking?" she said and he felt that she was trying to help him out a little bit. Like maybe she was no more a fan of Iris's visit to the sperm bank than he was.

"Is she at the fertility clinic?"

"I didn't tell you that."

"Understood. What time's her appointment?"

She squeezed her eyes shut. "What are you going to do?"

"Nothing. Try and talk her out of it before it's too late."

She glanced up at the big ceramic clock Iris's mother had given her for her birthday. The night he and she first made love. It said four-ten.

"I think you might already be too late."

"What time was her appointment?"

"Four."

"Directions?"

"You didn't get this from me."

"Noted. Come on! You don't want her to do this either. Give me the damn directions."

She gave him the damn directions. Then said, "Good luck."

He nodded. Ran out of the door, the foolish bells laughing at him as he exited.

Chapter Twenty-One

The clinic was easy to find. By four-twenty he was running into the clinic like a crazy man. All he could think was that every medical professional he'd ever consulted had made him wait. It was like they taught a whole course in med school on how long you should make patients wait.

But to his horror a quick glance around the waiting room showed two women pretending to read magazines. Neither of them was Iris.

He walked up to the desk and an attractive, slim woman who looked past the age of child rearing asked, "Can I help you?"

"I'm looking for Iris Chance," he said.

"She's not here."

"But her appointment was for four o'clock." He hoped if he offered information the woman would believe he actually knew Iris.

"I know. But she's gone."

For a second he could only stare stupidly at the woman as it dawned on him that he was too late.

He turned blindly for the door, mumbling something that might have been, "Thanks," but didn't sound like anything but an incoherent stammer.

He stepped outside onto the sidewalk and simply stood there. The day had been bright but now was cooling off. The few people on the street weren't dawdling. They were striding purposefully to wherever they were headed.

Nancy Warren

If he had a clue where he was headed, maybe he'd be moving quickly too. Instead he felt stuck here. Turned to stone. Outside a fertility clinic of all places.

He felt like he'd been kicked, and hard. The thought of driving home held no appeal. Truthfully, not much did. He hunched into his jacket, pushed his hands in his pockets and started walking. No idea where he was going. Just walking.

The medical office gave way to a dental clinic, then a cosmetic place offering something called a non-surgical facelift, then a drug store, and a yoga studio with an organic juice counter.

He kept walking. He thought if he hit a bar he'd be tempted to head on in and have a beer. Watch whatever sport was on the big screen.

He passed an organic grocer and next to it was a coffee shop. He glanced idly in the window and then stopped dead.

Iris was sitting alone at a table with a cup of coffee in front of her. Unlike every other patron in there, she had no companion, no book, no newspaper, computer, smart phone or other electronic device in front of her. She was staring at the cup of coffee almost as though she were planning to have a dialogue with it.

For a second he thought he was seeing things, but no, that woman with the long hair tied back, the flowered top, jeans and boots, the face that lit up his world, that was his Iris.

He walked inside and headed to where she was sitting.

She glanced up and her eyes widened.

He didn't have any idea what he was going to say, but words came out of his mouth.

"I don't care," he said.

"Pardon?"

"I don't care." Realizing that he was maybe talking a little on the loud side and other people were beginning to notice, he sat in the empty chair across from her.

"What are you doing here?" A delicate blush suffused her cheeks and he wondered if she could already have that pregnant glow people talked about. He'd never seen her look prettier.

"I tried to stop you. I went to the clinic but I was too late. I—" He felt the tiredness, the emotional fatigue and the shock of finding out that all his crazy rush to get his divorce hadn't made a damn bit of difference. "I wanted to stop you."

Her eyes seemed big and mysterious and yet as familiar as his own face in the mirror. How was that possible? And how could you love someone this much knowing she'd done something that would forever change your view of your life?

He had no idea. Love, like life itself, was sometimes more mystery than he liked.

"Why?" she asked.

There were fifty things he could say but only one thing that mattered. "Because I'm in love with you."

If anything her eyes grew larger and more luminous. He could never describe them and all the poets he'd read and studied and taught over the years couldn't come close to describing the beauty of Iris as he saw her now.

"You're in love with me?"

"Yes. And hell if I know why. You're impatient, misguided, so busy listening to everyone else's problems that you won't face your own, you won't even try to trust me, are probably pregnant right now with another man's child and I don't care." He stopped to breathe.

177

"You don't care if I'm pregnant with another man's child?"

It was slightly irritating that she kept repeating what he'd said but at least it proved she was listening to him.

"Of course I care. That should be my baby. Our baby. But I can't stop loving you. That is never going to happen."

She pushed her barely touched coffee aside and since her hands were out on the table top he took them in his. They were cold, he noticed. He wanted to wrap her in warmth and take care of her.

She didn't pull away which he figured was a good sign. In fact, her fingers trembled a little. "What are you saying?"

"What? Am I speaking Dutch? I love you. Iris, I want to marry you."

"But you're—"

"No. I'm not." Finally he could put an end to that objection. "I am not married. Okay, that isn't all the way true but I am as close to divorced as it is possible to be without holding a gun to a judge's head and forcing him or her to sign the decree."

She made a sound like a sob. "I thought you went back to your wife."

He felt the astonishment at her words knew it must show on his face. "Go back to my wife? Why would I ever do that? After what we've had together? When I'm in love with you?"

She shook her head. Clung to his hands. He could see extra shine in her eyes where he though she was trying not to cry. "I went to your place. On Saturday. I took over coffee and your favorite muffins. I was going to talk to you. The cat was hanging around looking for you too, and then your neighbor came out and said you'd gone to LA. What else was I supposed to think?"

"That I was going to get divorced? How about that? I left school at three o'clock on Thursday and drove to LA. That's a sixteen hour drive if you're interested. I had a couple of hours of sleep and then met with my lawyer and we had a really wonderful time meeting with my ex-wife who is of course represented by my ex best friend."

"That must have hurt." In spite of herself he could see her need to make him feel better surfacing.

"It did hurt. But only because I realized how stupid I'd been ever to marry someone I didn't really love. Maybe they'll be happy together. I hope so."

Her eyes widened. "You do?"

He grinned. "When I first found out they were together I hoped she'd gain four hundred pounds and his dick would fall off. But I've had some time away. And I met you. Now I try to be the bigger man and wish them well."

"Very Zen master of you."

He released her hands and pulled his copy of the settlement agreement out of his pocket. He flipped to the page where he and his ex had both signed it. "That's the agreement. Iris, it's done. All but some bureaucratic paperwork. My marriage is over."

She glanced at the paperwork he pushed her way. Touched his signature with her fingertip. "You drove for thirty-two hours over three days."

"I felt like you needed a grand gesture. I had to find a way to make you believe that I am never going back. I'm not on the rebound. This isn't a transitional relationship. I don't want to date and sleep with a bunch of women. I want you. I love you."

"Oh, Geoff."

"I admit the timing sucked. But when you meet the woman of your dreams, you don't turn away from such luck."

Her smile was sweet and warm. One of the first things he'd ever noticed about her. "I'm the woman of your dreams?"

He nodded. "What do you say? Will you take a chance and marry me?"

"You'll marry me even if I'm pregnant?"

He lifted her hands, clasped them in his once more. "I will."

She huffed a breath in and out and he felt her trying not to cry. Finally she said, "I never believed any man could love me this much. You know, in my life, I think somehow I got the feeling that I was never quite good enough. Oh, I was the woman that men told their troubles to, and leaned on in times of need. But I think I've always believed I have to be strong and hold it together. I can't lean on anyone."

"You can lean on me. I promise."

She nodded slowly. "I think I can."

He tugged on her hand. "Let's get out of here." When she rose he put an arm around her and said, close to her ear, "I need to kiss you very badly and I'm not doing it here."

Chapter Twenty-Two

When they got outside, Geoff was as good as his word. He pulled her to him and kissed her so long and so hard that her legs started to feel weak.

When he pulled away she saw, finally saw, the love shining in his face. In the deepest part of her she knew everything was going to turn out right.

"There's something I need to tell you," she said, feeling so much joy she thought she might burst with it.

"You love me too?" He linked his hand with hers and they headed off in the opposite direction to the fertility clinic.

"I do love you," she said, finally admitting the truth to him. "Oh, and it feels so good to say that out loud to you. I love you." She had to stop as he pulled her to him once more and kissed her until she giggled and pulled away. "But there's something else I need to tell you."

"That you'll marry me?"

She kissed him this time. "I will marry you. But not right this second. I think we need some time. My dad told me that I rush into things too often. He's right." She drew in a deep breath. "I trust and believe in you, in us. Let's take the time to be a couple. I want to plan a wedding."

He groaned. "Tell me it won't be in a ballroom with three hundred guests?"

"No." She was horrified. "Is that what your first wedding was like?"

"Nightmare."

"I was thinking a garden wedding. Marguerite will do the flowers. Dosana and I will do the catering. I think we should wait until Evan and Caitlyn get married. Maybe we could marry in September? No. Late August, so we can have a honeymoon before the school year starts again."

"I will marry you any day, anywhere you say."

"Oh, that is so good to hear."

"I feel like we should celebrate. Can I take you to dinner?" He pulled her against him and she thought she'd never get tired of feeling his warm, strong body against hers. In bed, walking on the street, pushing a stroller, anywhere at all. "We'll have champagne." Then he glanced down at her looking concerned. "Oh, I guess you can't drink, huh? If you're pregnant?"

She sighed out a huge puff of happy.

"I'm not pregnant." She stopped dead, turning him so they were looking at each other face to face. "I cancelled my appointment today."

"You mean, no turkey baster?"

"They do not use a turkey baster. And yes, I decided not to have the procedure after all."

"Why?" He was looking at her as though her next words would be the most important ones he ever heard. So she tried to give them to him.

"Because I love you." She knew they were the right words when he pulled her in for another of those leg weakening kisses. When they came up for air, she said, "I got to the door and I knew I couldn't let you go. I needed to give us a chance. To tell you how I felt. So, I figured, we'd talk and I'd see how you felt and, well, the sperm's frozen. It's not going anywhere."

His face, the face she was growing to love more each day, glowed with the news. Then his expression grew serious. In a firm tone, he said, "Let me be absolutely clear. That sperm is never going anywhere near you. I will be taking care of any inseminating that goes on in your body."

She shouldn't feel a rush of sexual excitement at a word like inseminating, but she did all the same. The idea of getting pregnant with Geoff was as sexy as anything she could imagine.

God, she loved him. How had she almost messed up so badly?

Now that she knew he loved her, now that she had enough self-confidence to believe him, she could tease. "I'll have you know that sample was expensive. Also, it was a birthday gift from my sister."

"Haven't you ever heard of regifting?"

She couldn't help but laugh. "This isn't a set of towels that don't fit your décor."

"I know. It's the possibility of a new life. And I'll bet there is an infertile couple somewhere who don't have a lot of money, who would love that sperm. I'll bet your sister could take care of it."

"You think I should regift sperm?"

"I do."

She kissed him. "I think that is a brilliant idea."

They walked on and then she found herself pausing. "You know, the reason I was fixated on having a baby is that my fertility might be compromised. There's a possibility that I won't be able to have kids."

"Honey, haven't you figured out yet that I'm all in? I love you. I'd love to have kids with you. I would. But if it's not in the cards, then we'll figure it out."

"I love you." She glanced up. "Have I said that too many times? It's like it snuck out and now I keep repeating myself."

"Some things never get old."

And he pulled her against him and kissed her while the future stayed firmly in the future and she let herself enjoy this perfect moment.

The End

If you enjoyed Iris in Bloom, please consider leaving a review and check out the other novels from the Take a Chance series!

KISS A GIRL IN THE RAIN
Take a Chance, Book One

In this sexy, humorous contemporary romance, a lost dog brings together a wealthy drifter and a small town doctor and changes all their lives forever.

Evan Chance is a man out to complete the bucket list he made as a kid, starting with ride a motorcycle across America. Caitlyn Sorenson is the sexy country doctor standing in his way. Or is she the dream he's been searching for?

When Evan Chance gives up a successful corporate law career to tackle the bucket list he wrote when he was twelve, he has no idea where the road will lead him.

Caitlyn Sorenson is a happily settled small town doctor. When a sexy drifter rolls into town after a motorcycle accident leaves him stranded in Miller's Pond for a few days with the homeliest dog ever, she can smell trouble even as she's drawn to a man who is only passing through town.

But some scorching hot nights and a blooming tenderness mean two people will have to face up to the challenges of love.

BLUEPRINT FOR A KISS
Take a Chance, Book Three

You can design a perfect life, then a woman comes along and messes it all up!

Prescott Chance is the go-to architect for the wealthy and famous, which has made him more wealthy and famous than he's ever wanted to be. He turns down more commissions than he accepts and is extremely private. Holly Legere is barely making ends meet between rent and student loans. As an assistant to Alistair Rupert, the notoriously difficult industrialist, she works night and day for slave wages, hanging on in hopes of a promised promotion in his huge organization. When Alistair Rupert's wife decides she wants a Prescott Chance designed house, and Prescott turns her down, it's Holly's job to make the choosy architect change his mind. And Holly is a very determined woman. In this modern romantic comedy, she'll go to any lengths to get him to design her boss a house, including pulling in his huge family for support. This is the third book in the Take a Chance series, though the books stand alone.

CHANCE ENCOUNTER
Take a Chance, Prequel

Daphne and Jack meet on a Greyhound bus heading north from California. The year is 1976 and Daphne is a pregnant teenager. Jack is a guy in search of a future. For these two lost souls, this is a ride that will change their lives and begin a dynasty. This is a prequel to the Take a Chance series about the eleven kids Jack and Daphne will collect over the years and the paths each member of this very untraditional family, will take as they, in turn, fall in love.

Other Books by Nancy Warren

WILD RIDE
A Changing Gears: Book 1

Duncan Forbes is a bad-boy adventurer, a motorcycle-riding art professor whose side hustle is tracking down stolen works of art, no matter what the danger, and restoring them to their rightful owners for a nice commission. When he rolls into the sleepy town of Swiftcurrent, Oregon, trouble rolls in with him.

Alexandra Forrest is a dedicated librarian. She's also a sexy woman who loves to wear high heels and tight clothes while she's shelving books. She dislikes the sexy drifter who saunters into her library on sight. When she stumbles over a dead body in her library the next day, she's pretty sure it's no coincidence. What follows is a Wild Ride that will challenge Alex and Duncan and shake up this sleepy town.

FAST RIDE
A Changing Gears: Book 2

Wes Doman is a biker with amnesia. Part of a notorious M/C gang that's terrorizing the town.
Or is he?
Nell Tennant is staying with her great Aunt Gertie in Harleyville. She's a refugee from a fast life in LA looking for some peace and quiet.
Or is she?
Changing Gears is the world famous bike store in Harleyville where the owner, a wizened old biker, says some things that make no sense.
Or do they?

Fast Ride is a sexy, humorous romance where a bad boy biker may have amnesia but he hasn't forgotten how to please his woman. Where the woman who he thinks is his isn't, and where nothing makes sense but the scorching intimacy between these two.

CRAZY RIDE
A Changing Gears: Book 3

Who's really crazy? Joe Montcrief is a hard driving workaholic corporate shark who rarely sees the light of day between the Manhattan highrises where he lives to work. When he arrives in the small town of Beaverton, Idaho with takeovers and profit in mind, he discovers the townspeople are eccentric to say the least and more interested in their slow pace of life than money. Sexy, gorgeous Emily Sargent runs the Shady Lady B&B, a former brothel where he's forced to stay as it's the only accommodation in town. The Shady Lady is so antiquated the only place he can get decent cell reception is in the middle of Emily's rose garden. Still, he manages to keep his mind on work except when Emily's around and he notices that this rose-growing, cookie baking, small-town girl has something about her that turns him inside out.

This small town, sexy contemporary romance, is a story where opposites attract and friends become lovers. Where it's never too late for old love or too fast for new love. In Beaverton, nothing is ever quite what it seems. And the citizens wouldn't have it any other way.

About the Author

Nancy Warren is the USA Today bestselling author of more than fifty novels. She continues to write for Harlequin Blaze as well as writing Indie books. Nancy is known for her sexy, humorous stories. She lives in the Pacific Northwest though she tends to wander. She is an avid hiker, a lover of good chocolate, good wine, and good stories.

Sign up for Nancy's Newsletter to keep up with her new releases and insider information she shares only with her newsletter subscribers. Subscribers also receive the chocolate chip cookie recipe from *The Christmas Grandma Ran Away from Home.*

Sign up through her website at www.nancywarren.net

Get in Contact with Nancy at:
www.facebook.com/nancy.warren.9655
twitter.com/NancyWarren1

Made in the USA
Lexington, KY
08 March 2019